THE ESSENCE

A Ghost Story in Three Days

Written by Vel Grande

Illustrations by Krystle Carkeek

12/2021

Danielle,
There's no such
place,
So far away.

JAY (Vel)

The Essence (A Ghost Story in Three Days)

ISBN 978-0-9892430-4-9

TABLE OF CONTENTS

The Essence
Book I

Friday and the Magic Wand

Vel Grande

Illustrations by Krystle Carkeek

From Vel to Greg Falcinelli,
Promise kept!

To my little brother Kalel,
Love Krystle

"Whatever our souls are made of,
his and mine are the same . . ."

Emily Bronte, *Wuthering Heights*

Chapter 1
Pancakes for Breakfast

This is a ghost story. No matter how old you get, the thought of ghosts in the dark is frightening. The feeling of your heart racing. Wondering whether you should run or hide. Grown-ups call it adrenaline. Fight or flight. But that is their adult way of saying they are scared. They are frightened of the dark. And like you, grown-ups believe in ghosts.

This is also a story of three days in the lives of three children alone at home for a weekend. For the sake of simple beginnings, their names are Alyssa, Bradley, and Sean. Their story began on a Friday morning when Alyssa Dempsey awoke for a second time.

The first time was when her mom gave her a light shake at six o'clock in the morning. John and Leslie Dempsey planned to celebrate their twentieth wedding anniversary at a small bed and breakfast in the Pocono Mountains in Pennsylvania, a four-hour ride from the Dempsey home, leaving Alyssa in charge of her two brothers.

Now you may wonder why two sensible parents – John and Leslie were certainly prudent people – would leave three children home alone for three days. The answer resided in their seventeen-year-old daughter Alyssa, a responsible straight-A student whom they previously left in charge of her brothers for their overnight getaways.

What was one more night? reasoned her father in proposing the weekend.

After speaking with Alyssa, Leslie booked the vacation. But Friday morning found Mrs. Dempsey a little nervous about leaving her daughter in charge for an extra day.

"Are you sure you'll be okay?" she whispered in the early morning darkness.

"We'll be fine," said Alyssa, eyes half-open. "You guys have a good time."

Leslie's question slightly annoyed Alyssa. Her track record was excellent, and she was more responsible than many of her friends' parents.

"Okay," said her mother. "We'll both have our cell phones on. I'll call tomorrow just to check in. And don't let Bradley give you a hard time."

The one guarantee for the weekend was that Alyssa's thirteen-year-old brother Bradley – he preferred Bradley, not Brad – would be a problem. Leaving Bradley with a babysitter, a grandparent, Alyssa, or anyone else always gave Leslie heart palpitations. One could use a lot of words to describe Bradley. Challenging, stubborn, demanding. They added up to a difficult boy. But if confronted with adversity, Leslie felt certain that Bradley's soul would stand and fight for his family.

"If for any reason you find yourself getting really angry at him, just do what I do. Close your eyes, take a deep breath, and count backward from ten."

"I will," Alyssa replied with a yawn. After receiving a soft kiss on her forehead, Alyssa fell back to sleep, dreaming of a friend's party.

While she slept, her youngest brother's blue eyes snapped open. Sean's night had been rather unusual, and he still held what his new friends left for him. It reminded

Sean of the long, thin plastic wand the magician used at his fourth birthday party the previous month. But this wand was made of glass with a dark red liquid trapped inside that moved when Sean turned it in his hand, which he did for a very long time until he heard Alyssa's cell phone play a musical ringtone across the hall.

The rising summer sun streamed through her window as Alyssa reached for the phone. She saw Sean emerge from his room twisting his fingers through the sandy curls of his hair. In his other hand, the little boy carried something that refracted the light passing over her head. Evaporating rainbows dotted his path.

"Morning," said Sean with a small singsong voice before disappearing down the hall. Alyssa gave him a sleepy wave.

"Hey," she said, putting the phone to her ear.

"Hey back," replied the smooth, soothing voice of Alyssa's boyfriend, Will. "What are you doing?"

"I was sleeping."

"Sorry. Were you dreaming about me?"

"No," said Alyssa with a yawn and a stretch. "Actually, I was dreaming I was at Rebecca's house and there was a party going on, but I was supposed to be watching my brothers. I looked around, but I couldn't find them. Then you called."

"So I saved you," Will said happily.

"Sort of." While they spoke, Alyssa began her morning fight with her long, dark-brown hair, which was curly like Sean's, but without the luxury of being cute when in a state of disarray. "What are you up to? I thought you were abandoning me for your grandparents this weekend?"

"I am. But I have something for you first. Look out the window."

Jumping up, Alyssa whipped her blanket and sheets aside. Will leaned against their mailbox holding a huge bouquet of summer flowers, a collage of yellow, white and orange. Seeing her widen the blinds, he waved.

"You rat," Alyssa cried. "I look terrible." Will ended the call and started walking toward the Dempseys' front door, smiling up at his girlfriend. "Rat!" she repeated, banging her fists on the window.

Alyssa interrupted her race downstairs to perform a mirror check in the hall bathroom. What a mess, she thought. Her white t-shirt sported an egg-shaped, brown stain from the coffee ice cream she dripped on it the previous night while watching television. Her baggy, grey sweats, hiding the extra five pounds she wrestled to lose every summer, looked no better. And my hair, she lamented silently, using her hands in vain to make some sense of the chaos.

"Yuck," she said with exasperation as the doorbell rang, the chime echoing up the stairs.

All six feet of Will leaned in for a kiss as Alyssa opened the door. The sweet fragrance of the flowers, the earthy smell of Will's cologne, and the touch of his lips made Alyssa forget about her early morning looks for a moment, until Bradley bounded down the steps, clad in navy-blue boxer shorts and a white undershirt, singing "kissy, kissy, kiss, kiss."

"Get lost," said Alyssa, whipping her head around with a snarl. Bradley stuck out a big, red tongue, rolled his fierce, blue eyes, and then retreated to join Sean in the family room – or rather, to evict Sean from the family room.

"My parents are finally away for a full weekend and you're not going to be here," moaned Alyssa, as she returned to Will with pouty lips. He was the first boy she loved. Alyssa lived for his smile, curling up his right cheek, and his soft black hair falling to the neck, which she played with to Will's unending annoyance.

"Hey, I'm the one stuck visiting my grandparents. Anyway, I'm coming home early Sunday. I'll be over before your folks get back," he said, handing the bouquet to Alyssa.

"I love them," said Alyssa, smiling. But before she could say another word, Sean and Bradley began fighting, their shouts rumbling down the hall to the foyer.

"I got here first!"

"You can watch cartoons in the basement!"

"Alyssa, he's pushing me!"

Lowering her head, Alyssa growled. Will put his hand on her chin, lifted her face, and gave Alyssa a quick kiss. "I'll see you Sunday."

"What's going on?" yelled Alyssa, stomping into the family room. She separated her brothers, while Sean continued to push at Bradley through his sister's legs. "Mom and Dad are gone like two hours and you're already fighting."

"He can watch cartoons somewhere else," complained Bradley, holding up a large, white plastic sword, encrusted with bright red and blue beads. Bradley's angry eyes flicked back and forth between Sean, the bratty brother who usually spoiled his fun, and Alyssa, the bossy sister who took pleasure in his misery.

Bradley snapped his chin up. "Well," he asked in a cynical voice. "Who wins? Like I don't know that already."

Alyssa shook her head and crossed her arms. She was not ready to win a fight, and this fight was not worth winning. She turned with an apologetic smile to Sean and he looked to the carpet with defeat.

"C'mon buddy. I'll make you breakfast. What do you want?"

"Pancakes!" recovered Sean with a shout.

As Alyssa led her youngest brother into the kitchen, Bradley shook his fist in triumph. *Yes*, he thought. Hero Warrior *is mine*. The worn, lined, grey face of an aging king greeted him on the television.

"Who are you?" asked the old ruler in a deep, raspy voice.

Bradley knelt before the cartoon image, planting the plastic tip of his toy sword into the carpeted floor. "I am the Hero Warrior, your loyal servant," he declared.

"I want to be a serve ant," said Sean, seated at the Dempseys' large, dark walnut kitchen table. He turned to Alyssa. "Is a serve ant bigger than a regular ant?"

"A servant is not an ant," explained Alyssa. "A servant is someone that has to do what another person tells them. All the time."

"I don't want to be that," Sean replied with a frown. "Can you make Bradley be my servant?"

"Never," shouted Bradley, overhearing his brother, while he danced about in a virtual battle.

Alyssa ignored them both. As Sean watched his sister search the cabinets for pancake mix, he played with the wand and wondered if his friends would bring him something else tonight.

"What's that?" asked Alyssa, recognizing the glass object Sean was carrying when Will called earlier.

"My magic wand," said Sean proudly. "See." He twirled it in his hand to show her. From the family room, Bradley cried "die, die!" with his sword flailing at unseen enemies.

"Will you shut up?" shouted Alyssa. Bradley disregarded her. "Where did you get it?" asked Alyssa, resuming her search.

"The Buddies gave it to me," explained Sean.

The hunt was not going well. No pancake mix yet. Sean was probably going to be disappointed. "Yeah," said Alyssa. "And who are the Buddies?"

"My friends. I saw them last night. They gave me this."

"Yeah," replied Alyssa, barely listening. "Speaking of buddies, buddy, I don't see any pancake mix."

"But I want pancakes!"

Looking at the cabinets with defeat, Alyssa scratched her head. "How about eggs?"

"No. I want pancakes. Blueberry pancakes, and strawberry pancakes, and banana pancakes, and chocolate chip pancakes, and . . ."

"Sean," interrupted Alyssa, raising her voice. She peered into the last cabinet. "Sorry buddy, but it doesn't look like I'm making pancakes this morning."

"You don't have to," said Sean. "We have lots and lots already."

The warm, sweet smell reached Alyssa's nose. The smell of . . .

Alyssa turned around and reached back to hold herself up. Sean smiled, waving the wand with glee. In front of him, covering the table, were stacks of pancakes. Hundreds were piled high with sugar-scented steam rising off of them, curling away into the air.

Chapter 2
The Wand

"I have you now," shouted Bradley, darting about in the family room. Sniffing the pancakes, but unaware of what was happening in the kitchen, Bradley added, "Hey, they smell good. Save some for me!"

Alyssa remained frozen, propped up against the counter for support. She raised her trembling hands to her mouth.

"What did you do?" she whispered. "How did you make that happen?"

"I don't know," said Sean, beaming. "I just made them. I want a bicycle, too."

With a wave of the wand, the air seemed to twist. Where there was nothing, Sean's requested bicycle now stood, brand new, bright red, with a white stripe wrapped around the metal frame and balanced on the Dempseys' beige, ceramic kitchen floor with its stainless-steel kickstand extended.

"Yay," sang Sean. "I want a bell."

Alyssa's eyes detected the same momentary twist and suddenly there was a silver bell attached to the right handlebar. As with the bicycle, the bell did not appear slowly. It was as if it had always been there and was simply overlooked. Alyssa thought to scream, but that was one thought of thousands racing through her mind, including stopping Sean as he waved the glass wand again.

"Ring!"

The bell began ringing, its tiny white, plastic handle repeatedly snapped forward by some invisible thumb insistent on filling the kitchen with a jingling clamor. Bradley raced in from the family room. Alyssa moved her hands from her mouth, placing them protectively on her ears.

"Stop it, Sean," cried Alyssa over the racket. "Stop it!"

"Stop," yelled Sean, silencing the bell. Alyssa pounced. She rushed her youngest brother and snatched the wand from his hand.

"Hey," he complained. "That's mine."

"What's with the pancakes? What's with the bike? What's with the bell?" demanded Bradley.

Alyssa ignored him and studied the slippery, glass wand. She lifted it toward the kitchen's sunlit bay window, and the wand refracted the light as it had earlier that morning when she glimpsed it in Sean's hand. Rolling it between her fingers, the wand felt uneven. Along its length there were long, thin facets which intersected at odd angles, as if the glass was carelessly carved.

"What is it?" asked Bradley.

"It's a magic wand," replied Sean. "And it's mine. Not yours. Mine."

"A magic wand?" Bradley said with disbelief. "I don't think so."

"Well, think so," exclaimed Alyssa. "He just made all of this out of thin air! The pancakes, the bike, and the bell!"

Trying to make sense of the situation, Bradley looked around at Sean's creations, while Alyssa raised the wand to her eyes. Inside was a dark, red liquid. *Maybe it's red mercury*, she thought. She slowly turned it in her hand, moving the liquid back and forth. The fluid did not slide in a line, but expanded and contracted throughout the wand.

Is it breathing? wondered Alyssa. *Is it alive?*

"Sean," Alyssa said sternly, her voice quivering a bit. "Where did you get this?"

"I told you," replied Sean. "The Buddies gave it to me."

Bradley Dempsey, his brain dancing with a wealth of possibilities, did not care about the origin of the wand. "It doesn't matter!" he shouted. "We can wish for whatever we want!"

Alyssa's mouth dropped open. "Are you crazy?"

"I want *Hero Warrior 2*. Wish for *Hero Warrior 2*! Please Alyssa, wish for it," begged Bradley.

She turned to Sean. Half of a blueberry pancake hung from his mouth. Alyssa waited for Sean to finish and swallow, while Bradley dropped to his knees continuing to plead his case.

"How did you wish for all of this?" she asked Sean.

He rolled his eyes. "I told you that, too. I just made them."

"I know," Alyssa said slowly. "But what did you do to make them?"

Sean's small, pink tongue licked a spot of blueberry juice from his top lip while he considered the question. *How did I make them*?

Sean studied the pancakes. One of the blueberries looked like an insect with a big, black head. Yesterday, he saw a black and red stink bug crawling on their driveway. Sean considered stepping on it, but squished stink bugs smelled bad. Maybe he would go outside after breakfast to look for it. *I can wish for the bug*, Sean thought with a smile.

"What?" he asked.

"Sean," Alyssa said patiently. "What did you do to make the pancakes and the bicycle?"

"Who cares?" repeated Bradley, driving his face between

Alyssa and Sean. "Just make a wish!"

"Shut up!" screamed Alyssa. Bradley backed away, mumbling to himself in anger. Alyssa composed herself and took a breath. "Sean?"

Her little brother lifted his shoulders while he played with his curly hair. "I don't know. I said I wanted them. Can I ride my bike now?"

"Not yet." Alyssa paced around the kitchen. *I should call Mom and Dad*, she thought. She felt overwhelmed and part of her wanted to run back upstairs, get under the covers and convince herself that this was a dream.

Bradley pulled out a kitchen chair and plopped down with a thump. He picked up a chocolate chip pancake and shoved the whole thing in his mouth.

"Eww," remarked Sean.

"You know what I'd do," said Bradley, his stuffed mouth muffling his voice. "Not that anyone listens to me around here. I'd test it out."

"Test it out?" asked Alyssa. "How?"

"Don't go overboard like pancake-bicycle boy. You should wish for . . . hmmm. Wish for an apple."

Alyssa squeezed the wand. *An apple? That's a good test.* But then she thought about a car. She desperately wanted her own car.

What if I wished for a Volkswagen Beetle? Bright yellow with a cut sunflower in the dash, and Will next to me. We could go to the beach whenever we want.

"What are you doing?" asked Bradley, watching his sister think. "It's only an apple."

"An apple?" Alyssa repeated, emerging from her fantasy.

Her brothers both nodded. Alyssa raised the wand and pointed it toward the kitchen counter. Narrowing her eyes, she flicked her wrist and said, "I want an apple."

Nothing. All three Dempseys looked around, floor to ceiling. Pancakes. Bicycle with a bell. But no apple.

Bradley got up and approached Alyssa, his hand held open. “Let me try.”

Any moment spent trusting Bradley was a moment his sister regretted. Just the same, Alyssa handed him the glass wand to see what would happen.

Spinning in a circle, Bradley leapt and cried, “Alacron, alacron, biscuit-boy. I want an apple!” Gravity returned him with a thud to the ceramic tiled floor. Nothing.

Alyssa pursed her lips and crossed her arms. “Alacron, alacron, biscuit-boy?” She snatched the wand from Bradley’s hand.

“Me, me, me,” said Sean, raising his arm. “My turn.” Alyssa and Bradley eyed each other. Bradley nodded vigorously.

"*Hero Warrior 2,*" he whispered out of the side of his mouth to his little brother.

"Wish for an apple, Sean," warned Alyssa. "Not anything else. Understood?"

"Yes," said Sean.

Alyssa handed the wand back to him and held her breath. "I want a . . . purple apple," announced Sean. Once again, the light seemed to bend. As if conjured by the Wicked Witch for Snow White, there on the kitchen table, balanced upon the cooling pancakes, was a shiny, purple apple.

"I made it," said Sean, rejoicing.

Bradley began a celebratory dance. "This is going to be the best weekend ever! We can have anything we want. Ice cream. As much ice cream as we want. And a million dollars. And a new HDTV with 3-D," he said pointing to the family room. "And *Hero Warrior 2*!"

"Cut it out," barked Alyssa, seizing the wand. "We are not making any more wishes." Alyssa spoke to Bradley while pointing at Sean. "What if you annoy him and he wishes you were dead? So much for the best weekend ever."

Bradley eyed his brother. Sean flashed a rather devilish grin.

"Sean," said Alyssa in a patient tone. "Tell us about the Buddies giving you the wand. Tell us as much as you remember."

"They came to my room last night and gave me the wand." Alyssa and Bradley waited for more. Sean stared back. "That's it."

Alyssa shook her head. *This is like talking to Will,* she thought. No matter what age, boys did not understand the concept of details.

"What did they look like?"

Sean prepared to respond, when an idea struck him.

While Alyssa and Bradley watched silently, Sean took a clear drinking glass from the drying rack. Standing on the green, plastic footstool his mom placed by the sink, he filled the glass with water and put it back on the kitchen counter.

"What are you doing?" asked Bradley.

Sean ignored his brother. Instead, he opened the refrigerator and took out a half-full quart of milk. Returning to the countertop, he carefully poured a little of the milk into the water.

"They looked like that," said Sean.

Staring into the glass, Alyssa and Bradley watched the milk drift through the water, forming a shape that turned their skin cold.

It was a ghost.

Chapter 3
The Mirror

Sean Dempsey lived in a patchwork bedroom of his preschool icons. A Thomas the Tank Engine comforter covered his bed, a Spiderman sign imprinted with the words "Sean's Room" hung on the wall, and a large, stuffed Spongebob Squarepants dangled from the ceiling in the corner, no doubt the leader of the menagerie of cartoon characters and plush animals littered about the room.

The decorative chaos partly concealed Alyssa's old, hand-me-down, pickled-oak furniture set, which included Sean's bed, a night table, a chest of drawers topped with an assemblage of birthday party awards, a pee-wee soccer trophy, and a dresser adorned with a corkboard covered with a colorful gallery of Sean's art projects. Upon the dresser sat a matching, framed, rectangular mirror.

"Where did the Buddies come from?" asked Alyssa, leading the investigation, as the three siblings gathered in Sean's room.

Sean pointed at the white-bordered mirror and Bradley burst out laughing. "Oh, that is so *Alice in Wonderland*," he said sarcastically, and then turned to his sister. "We have the movie downstairs. He's watched it about fifty times. He probably dreamed it, or he's making it up."

"I did not make it up," yelled Sean, and he flashed his

right hand in anger at his brother. Bradley easily deflected the young boy's swat, and the two began shoving each other.

"Will you guys both stop it!" shouted Alyssa, separating them. She pushed Bradley backward a step and pointed the wand at him. "If he's dreaming, how does that explain this wand? How does it explain the pancakes? The bicycle? The purple apple?"

Although Bradley refused to admit it, Alyssa was probably right. But his father taught him to always look for the rational explanation. Last year the Dempsey house was in a similar panic about a ghost in their attic, until his dad came home. John Dempsey calmly led his family up the creaky attic steps and they soon discovered that the ghost was an owl.

"Wait," said Bradley, his eyes lighting up. "Dad works for the government. Maybe the wand is something from his job."

"I don't think so, brainiac," replied Alyssa. "Dad works for the Department of Agriculture."

"Exactly," responded Bradley with confidence. "Maybe they invented something to create food. That would explain the pancakes and apple. Who's the brainiac now?" he added, gloating.

Alyssa stared at Bradley. If the owner actually ended up being a ghost, she would happily propose trading her annoying brother for the wand. Rather than waste more time, she returned to Sean. Brevity was easier to deal with than foolishness.

"Tell me more about the Buddies and the wand."

Sean thought for a moment and then announced he was going to the bathroom. Two minutes later, the toilet flushed loudly and Sean was back in his room with Alyssa squeezing his hand somewhat forcefully, repeating her question. Before Sean could answer, Bradley piped in.

"Maybe it was aliens." Alyssa glared at her brothers. *Enough already*, she thought.

"Listen closely. I am going to kill one of you very soon. Now I am in charge, so both of you shut up!"

Bradley and Sean stood attentively, although Bradley did so reluctantly. Attempting to assert her authority, Alyssa's eyes darted back and forth between them, until finally falling on Sean. "Tell me more about the Buddies and the wand," she said deliberately.

Sean pointed at his mouth and made "mmm" sounds. "What's wrong now?" asked Alyssa in a weary voice.

"You told me to shut up," said Sean.

Alyssa collapsed to the floor on her knees and grabbed her little brother by his small, thin arms.

"Sean. I am going to start crying. You don't want to see me cry, do you?" He shook his head. "Good. Then please tell me about the Buddies and the wand."

Sean almost asked his sister what she wanted to know about the Buddies, but even at the age of four he intuitively sensed that might drive Alyssa into hysterics.

"They gave it to me," began Sean. "They told me to keep it safe and not to play with it. They said it was very special. And then they went back in there," he added, pointing at the mirror.

Fighting off a feeling of nausea, Alyssa imagined ghosts floating around in Sean's bedroom during the previous night, twenty or thirty feet from her bed.

"Tell me more, Sean. Tell me as much as you remember. How many were there? What did they look like?"

"They looked like ghosts . . . brainiac," interrupted Bradley in a mocking tone.

"They were sort of people-clouds," said Sean. Remembering them, he paused for a moment. His sister and Bradley seemed scared, but Sean liked the Buddies. *Spiders are scary,* he thought. *Super scary. But Mommy is not afraid of spiders. She kills them with a tissue. Even the big ones.*

Alyssa watched Sean glaze over. "This is impossible," she sighed, and she snapped her fingers in his face. "Sean!"

"Huh?" he asked. "Oh. People-clouds. But when they moved it was sort of moving by wind. Except, there was no whoosh noise."

They? Sean kept saying the word "they," and now Alyssa pictured a stream of floating ghosts pouring out of his mirror. "How many buddies were there, Sean?" she asked tentatively, holding her breath.

"Two," said Sean. Alyssa exhaled in relief. "One was a boy. He was funny. He made a silly face." Sean stuck his tongue out and wiggled his head around. Alyssa and Bradley looked at each other. Neither of them laughed.

"The other was a girl," continued Sean. "She gave me the wand and said I had to keep it safe. She seemed pretty smart, but I think she was afraid."

Safe from what, thought Alyssa. She hoped to avoid finding out. "How was she afraid?"

"She kept looking back at the mirror," replied Sean.

He wanted to tell his sister that the girl ghost was pretty. In his preschool class there was a girl named Ellie who made him feel happy when he looked at her. Ellie's eyes were emerald green and Sean loved touching her red hair, which reminded him of strawberry fruit roll-ups against his white fingers. Sean liked the girl ghost the way he liked Ellie. But he thought Bradley would make fun of him if he said that.

"Do you know why she kept looking at the mirror?" asked Alyssa.

"I think she was scared," whispered Sean. "And I think maybe I saw something in there. Maybe there was another Buddy?"

Bradley strolled over to the mirror and stuck out his finger. "Don't touch it," hollered his sister, but he ignored her and tapped on the glass.

"See. No Buddies," said Bradley casually. "Just a mirror."

"But it was different last night," protested Sean. "It was like . . . like . . . water."

Bradley ran his finger down the glass, his skin squealing against the surface. "Doesn't feel like water to me."

"But it was different –"

“Shhh,” said Alyssa, calming Sean down. She turned to Bradley. “Stop provoking him! I am trying to find out what happened.”

“I still say he was dreaming,” replied Bradley, sticking out a big, red tongue at his sister.

Alyssa shook her head in disgust and returned to Sean. She held out the wand. The red liquid inside pressed forcefully against the glass shell. “What did they say you should do with this? How do you keep the magic wand safe?”

"She didn't call it a magic wand," remembered Sean. "She said it was a 'mess.' Or something with a 'mess' in it." Sean rubbed his eyes. "I'm getting tired."

With her free hand, Alyssa gave Sean an encouraging rub through the curls of his hair. "That's okay, buddy."

Realizing what she said, Alyssa turned to Bradley and mouthed the word "buddy" to him. "You see?" said Bradley.

Buddy. That's what Alyssa called Sean all of the time. She gazed at the glass wand. Was this about ghosts? Or magic? Or, were they all caught up in Sean's dream. She looked at Bradley, again. "But the pancakes? The bike? The apple?"

Bradley shrugged his shoulders. "I don't know."

On her knees by Sean, Alyssa got up and ran her hand through her tangled, brown hair, trying to clear the cobwebs of confusion. "Whatever is going on," she announced, "we probably won't get any answers until these Buddies come back. If they ever do."

"I know when they're coming back," said Sean with a wide, tooth-filled smile.

Alyssa's body stiffened. Sean's blue eyes beamed with excitement, and she knew immediately the question she would ask and the answer her brother would give. Alyssa shut her eyes and offered a prayer.

Let it all be a dream, please, she thought. *Let it all be a dream. Bring Mom and Dad home, and make it safe. Please.*

"I know when they're coming back," repeated Sean through the buzzing in Alyssa's brain.

"When are they coming back?"

"Tonight," announced Sean. "They said they would check on me tonight."

Chapter 4
The Vigil

Lying in bed, Alyssa watched the burnt-orange light of dusk filling her room. Earlier, she responded to her little brother's news of the Buddies' impending arrival by fainting. Now, a different and far more ominous darkness was arriving.

Across the hall, she heard Sean playing and singing a song which did nothing to ease her fear of the coming night.

You are my buddies
You are my friends
You are my buddies
You remember me
and I remember you

Alyssa rolled to her side, keeping a tight grip on Sean's magic wand. Reflecting the color of her room, the glass wand was also tinted auburn, lit by the scattered rays of the setting sun. But Alyssa could make out the blood red substance within, still churning back and forth.

She examined the liquid several times after regaining consciousness, trying to find a clue as to how it produced pancakes and a bicycle on her little brother's command. Often the red fluid looked like it was going to leak out of the glass, spraying inside the ends of the wand. At other times the liquid formed into thick bubbles, creating images.

Alyssa stared intently at one of the larger bubbles and

thought she saw a man's face, but it quickly vanished. Another bubble appeared and her breath cut short. It was Sean, but then he too was gone.

Alyssa shook her head, convinced she was seeing things. Hours earlier, lying on the floor of Sean's bedroom with tear-sized droplets of water dribbling down her face, Alyssa opened her eyes and found Bradley holding an empty glass, having dumped its contents upon her.

"Was it a dream?" Alyssa asked her brothers with a hopeful smile. They both shook their heads. No.

Alyssa's cell phone chimed, announcing a new text message. The phone lay next to her alarm clock, which silently blared out the numbers 8:30 in bright, neon red. Night was no longer coming. Night had arrived.

She picked up her phone and read the message from Will.

HAVING FUN? I LOVE YOU.

Alyssa quickly sent a text back. I LOVE YOU TOO. Then she held the phone for a moment more and again considered contacting her parents.

I should call them, she thought. The problem was explaining the emergency. What would she say? Mom. Dad. Sean has a magic wand pancake-maker given to him by two ghosts. But what if something happened to Sean or Bradley? Her parents would never forgive her. *I could never forgive myself.*

Getting up, Alyssa walked across the hall and watched Sean. He was on the floor with a pad of construction paper and a cluster of pastel-colored crayons scattered around him, drawing pictures of ghosts while he sang:

You are my buddies
You are my friends
You are my buddies

You remember me
and I remember you

The last two lines struck Alyssa as odd. “How do the Buddies remember you Sean?” she asked.

“From last night,” he replied, his head facing down while he crayoned.

Alyssa intended to press the point, but then what was the point? Her little brother was four years old. He was too busy having fun to worry.

“Did they sing that to you?”

“Nope,” replied Sean. “I made it up. What do you think of my pictures? I used yellow for the Buddies because you can’t see white on white paper.”

Sean held one up with a ghost that looked more like a plump, gold snowman without the carrot nose.

"They're nice," said Alyssa, forcing a smile. "Do you know when the Buddies will come back?"

"Sooooon," responded Sean, stretching the word in a silly but spooky voice that completely creeped Alyssa out. "Can I have my wand?" he asked.

"Not yet, little man," said Alyssa. For now, she was going to call Sean "little man" rather than "buddy."

Alyssa walked down the hall to discover Bradley in his bedroom scampering around, fighting unseen enemies with his plastic *Hero Warrior* sword. Unlike Sean's room, Bradley Dempsey lived in a world crammed with death and violence. Action pictures of professional wrestlers covered the walls, complemented by posters of video game soldiers. The most prominent figure was the medieval Hero Warrior himself, arms rippling with muscles as he plunged his cold, steel blade into a fierce, green-bodied dragon.

"What are you doing?" she asked.

Bradley stopped his imaginary battle and assumed a military pose with the point of his sword pressed into the carpeted floor. "I'm practicing. We may have to fight the Buddies."

Alyssa rolled her eyes. "You are going to fight ghosts with a piece of molded plastic?" she asked incredulously.

"Maybe it will scare them," Bradley shot back. "At least I'm thinking ahead."

Am I the only sane person in this house? wondered Alyssa. Sean eagerly awaited the return of his ghost friends, while Bradley planned to drive them away with a toy sword. Bringing her parents in on the day's events was definitely the responsible choice.

"I'm calling Mom and Dad," she said.

"What?" cried Bradley. "You can't."

"I can and I'm going to," Alyssa replied.

Bradley grabbed his sister's arm as she turned away. "Wait. Look, if you call them now they're going to think it's a joke, or maybe we're crazy, or maybe worse they'll call weirdo Mrs. Watson next door and we'll have to go over her house with all of her smelly cats for the night."

Bradley's words stopped Alyssa. Estelle Watson was a lonely widow that lived next to the Dempseys and babysat the children for years until Alyssa was old enough to assume the job. And that was a happy day for her and Bradley, both of whom felt the urge to run while in the old woman's presence. To be fair, Mrs. Watson was rather harmless, quietly tending to her trio of indoor cats and her cherished garden of red rosebushes. However, to a child . . .

"She is scarier than a ghost," added Bradley.

Alyssa took a long breath and wavered. "One night," she said to Bradley, but Alyssa instantly felt that the new course of action was a mistake. "Just tonight. And if anything strange happens, I'm calling Mom and Dad for sure. Even if it's three in the morning."

"Awesome," shouted Bradley, raising his sword in the air. "The battle between good and ghosts is on!"

Thirty minutes later, Alyssa and her brothers were back in Sean's room. Wearing green plaid shorts and a black t-shirt, Bradley arrived with a juvenile armory, including his *Hero Warrior* sword, a plastic axe, a toy machine gun untouched since he was nine, and a Viking helmet.

With her index finger, Alyssa evicted him from the room. "Get that stuff out of here," she demanded. "I have enough to worry about without preventing you from attacking whatever it is we're waiting for."

Bradley complained bitterly, but to no avail. Finally, when Alyssa threatened to have him wait in the hall, rather than in Sean's bedroom, he stomped off to disarm. After

Bradley returned, Sean found both his brother and sister looking at him quizzically.

"What?"

"You tell us," said Alyssa.

Sean scanned his room. The Buddies would not expect to find three people in his bed, so he thought it was better if they sat on the floor, or maybe in the corner. Or maybe they could get the big, green tent they sometimes set up in the backyard. Sean remembered last summer when he and Bradley were in the tent, watching a baby skunk and its mother dig for grubs in the lawn.

"Sean!" yelled his sister. "Focus!"

"Oh. I think it should be dark," said Sean.

Holding her breath, Alyssa turned off the lights and the three siblings crowded in the corner of the room opposite Sean's empty bed. On his night table, the bright blue numbers of Sean's clock cast an eerie glow.

8:47.

They sat in silence staring at the mirror. Sean smiled cheerfully, wondering what the Buddies would bring him tonight. He really wanted a kite. Bradley gritted his teeth, readying himself for combat and angry that his sister deprived him of his sword. Alyssa felt numb as she sat wide-eyed, scanning the mirror for any sign of movement. In it, she could see the backward reflection of half of the "Sean's Room" Spiderman sign.

8:52.

"Where are they?" asked Bradley, breaking the stillness.

"Shut up," whispered Alyssa forcefully, momentarily startled by the sound of her brother's voice. "Sit still and be quiet."

"Sit still and be quiet," mimicked Bradley.

Nine o'clock came. Then nine-thirty. The numbness Alyssa felt was slowly being replaced by cramping in her legs. Sean cuddled wearily into her lap. At ten o'clock, Alyssa could tell by his rhythmic breathing that Sean was asleep.

At ten-thirty Bradley got up and ran to the bathroom. While returning, he thought about grabbing his sword, but admirably decided not to antagonize his sister.

10:59.

As the numbers changed to eleven, Alyssa turned and saw Bradley's head starting to nod.

"Hey," she said in a low voice. Bradley snapped his head up. "Don't leave me by myself."

"Sorry," said Bradley.

Conversation might be the best way to keep her brother awake. "Why do you think only Sean can make stuff with the wand?" she asked. "And don't say something stupid."

"I don't know," replied Bradley with a long, open-mouthed yawn. "I was thinking about that too. Maybe it only works for wishes of really little kids."

"Maybe the Buddies gave him a special power or something," suggested Alyssa. She was so tired of thinking. "Or maybe it really is all a dream."

"If you're in my dream, it's a nightmare," said Bradley with a smile. His sister responded with a sarcastic, "Ha, ha, ha." And that ended their conversation.

Alyssa stared at the mirror while watching Bradley's head nods become more frequent. By midnight he was going under, and she was fighting to keep her eyelids apart. Taking Sean's little hand in hers, Alyssa leaned back against the wall. Maybe it was really all a dream.

* * *

3:42.

With a burst of adrenaline, Alyssa's eyes opened. Her entire body ached and she calculated that she probably sat in the same position for the last seven hours. Her brothers were out cold. Sean was glued to her torso, while Bradley tilted away from her with a tiny bit of drool hanging from the side of his mouth, tinted blue from the clock.

Alyssa squeezed her eyelids tightly and then opened them, this time examining the mirror. It seemed different, almost like a small pond shimmering in the darkness. She searched for the "Sean's Room" sign. It was on the wall, but not in the reflection. *There is no reflection*, she thought.

The glass had vanished.

Then the mirror appeared to change. Something bulged in the middle.

What is that? Alyssa wondered, getting ready to wake Bradley. She strained her eyes and then her breath caught in her throat.

A white, misty hand was coming through the mirror.

Chapter 5
The Buddies

Alyssa watched a hand, then an arm, then a face, and finally a body silently pass through the flowing boundary of Sean's mirror, until at last the entire ghost floated in mid-air, moving toward her little brother's bed.

It's a man, thought Alyssa, tracking his progress across the room with her eyes. She felt a mix of terror and fascination wash through the inside of her chest. The ghost was a flowing connection of wispy, white lines, shaded light blue by the numbers on Sean's clock. He appeared rather heavy, but moved effortlessly. And although the lines gave him substance, Alyssa could see objects in the room through his misty body as he passed them.

The ghost drifted toward Sean's bed and stopped. He examined the area, clearly looking for her brother. In a normal-sounding male voice, devoid of an eerie tone or inflection, he whispered her brother's name.

"Sean," he said, expecting a response from the unoccupied blanket and sheets. Alyssa's racing mind was unsure what to consider first – the fact that the ghost was referring to her brother by name, the idea of a talking ghost hovering a few feet away from her and her brothers, or the fear that at any moment it might turn its head without her having a plan as to how she would react. But all those thoughts vanished as another pale-white, supernatural face popped noiselessly through the mirror.

"Benny," it said softly, but forcefully, in a woman's voice. "What are you doing?"

Even in the blue-lit darkness, Alyssa was mesmerized. *She is beautiful*, thought Alyssa. The ghost's young face was thin with soft, white, misty angles defining her cheeks and chin. Her snowy eyes were wide and intent, with the right eye partially covered by strands of sheer, colorless hair.

"He's not here," answered Benny, turning to the woman.

With a hushed scowl, the other ghost emerged, joining Benny by Sean's bed. *She's in charge*, thought Alyssa.

For a moment her eyes lingered on the mirror. There appeared to be another figure floating beneath the surface. *A third one*, wondered Alyssa.

"Where is he?" the female ghost asked.

With a snort from his congested nose, Bradley shifted his position by Alyssa's side. "Where is who?" he replied, his voice thick with sleep.

Bradley turned to her with his eyes shut, but there was nothing Alyssa could say. No "Don't move." No "Be quiet." No words at all, and certainly nothing to distract her attention away from the two ghosts, their phantom heads twisting slowly around to catch sight of the three Dempsey children crouched in the corner of the bedroom.

Perhaps it was the pounding of their sister's heart, or perhaps it was the sudden stillness of her breath. No matter, something was wrong, dragging Bradley and Sean from sleep.

"Where is who?" repeated Bradley, his eyes opening and finding his sister's face fixed on something behind him. Similar to the ghosts, Bradley gradually turned his head, stopping at the gaze of two pairs of milky-white eyes. And that is when Sean Dempsey woke up.

"Buddies!" shouted Sean with a big smile.

The word hung over the bedroom for a moment before Bradley began to scream, a deep, guttural frightened scream one might make before being hit by a bus, or upon discovering a rattlesnake in one's bed, or when staring at the faces of two ghosts.

Bradley screamed. Benny the ghost screamed. Alyssa screamed. Then Bradley screamed louder. And next door, Mrs. Watson rolled over in her bed and dreamt of being trapped at a rock concert.

In a flash of white-blue mist, the ghosts fled from the bedroom, disappearing into the mirror.

"Come back," cried Sean, jumping up and running to his dresser.

The departure of Benny and his female companion quieted Alyssa, but did nothing to pacify Bradley. He continued drawing on an endless reserve of air, which fueled his yelling. Sean maintained his position in front of the mirror, calling for the Buddies to return.

"Shut up!" shouted Alyssa at Bradley, trying to end the racket emitting from his mouth. "They're gone!"

Bradley finished a last scream and finally fell silent, except for the hyperventilation replacing his cries. "They're gone," said Alyssa, taking the extraordinary step of putting her arm around Bradley's trembling shoulder. "You won the shrieking battle."

"Come back," pleaded Sean. With a sad, quivering bottom lip, he gazed into the black, shimmering mirror, which produced no reflection. "It's all quiet now."

Leaving Bradley's side, Alyssa crept forward, joining Sean. "The Buddies are in there," her little brother added.

The mirror was a twinkling, glistening pond filled with

thousands of tiny, little stars, floating beneath the surface. Leaning in, Alyssa could feel the air become cooler, caressing her sweaty face. She breathed deeply, a dry chill filling her nose and lungs.

"Careful," whispered Bradley, still rooted in the same spot behind his sister.

Alyssa drew even closer, focusing on the glimmering, shiny points. Clutching the wand, she lifted it to the mirror. The dots of light reacted, glowing stronger and more distinct in its presence. Maybe there was no third ghost. Maybe it was a luminous pattern created by the small lights.

They do look like stars, Alyssa thought. *Or diamonds. Or distant –*

The female ghost's face burst through. Alyssa retreated, grabbing Sean as she fell back to the floor. Struggling to scream, Bradley produced only a pitiful, mousy squeak.

"Where is the Essence?" she demanded, emerging from the mirror, staring intently at Sean with a pale, angry face. He quickly pointed at his sister. "Where is it?"

Alyssa searched for a voice. Realizing that "the Essence" was the wand, she thrust it into the air, a glass charm defending the ghost's onslaught.

"He was m-making pan-pancakes," she stammered.

Benny's face popped through. His eyes were wide and questioning. "Annie? Is it okay?"

Benny and Annie. Ghosts with names, thought Alyssa. *These are people. Or they were people.*

Annie ignored Benny and continued questioning Alyssa. "Pancakes?"

"He was wishing things with it," said Alyssa.

Annie frowned disapprovingly at Sean. "We told you it wasn't a toy. That you have to keep it safe."

"I'm sorry," said Sean. "I was just playing."

Benny reemerged and floated by Annie's side. "He was just playing," he said, defending Sean. "Nothing bad happened, did it?"

All three Dempsey children shook their heads. Benny spoke calmly, and his soft, puffy features balanced Annie's intensity. Recognizing a new friend, the Dempseys inched toward the big ghost.

Alyssa looked at Annie and summoned some courage. "What is it for?" she asked.

Annie's white eyes narrowed. Benny waited silently for her response. *She is definitely the one in charge*, thought Alyssa.

"That's not your concern," Annie said sternly. The matter was closed. "Make sure it's safe and keep it away from the mirror. And no more wishing, understood?"

The children nodded their heads.

"We'll be back tomorrow night," said Annie. She turned and soundlessly vanished into the mirror, leaving the Dempseys alone with Benny.

"Are you still my buddies?" asked Sean in a quiet voice.

"Of course we are, Sean," said Benny. "Would all of you like to see a magic trick?"

"I would," said Sean excitedly.

"Okay," said Alyssa and Bradley mechanically.

Benny flashed a big smile filled with transparent teeth. He waved a white hand in front of them and placed it behind his back. Through his translucent body, the children watched as he raised three fingers.

"Guess how many fingers I'm holding up?"

Alyssa and Bradley stared at him with blank expressions, but Sean smiled back. "I know," he shouted, beaming.

Annie's face pushed through the mirror. "Benny!"

Benny winked at the kids, and then disappeared with Annie across the shimmering, star-filled boundary.

"We have to tell someone," yelled Bradley, when the ghosts were gone. "We have to tell someone, now!"

Alyssa let go of her brothers and slowly rose to her feet. Free of his sister's protection, Sean leapt toward the dresser and began calling for the Buddies to return.

"We have to tell someone," yelled Bradley, jumping in front of Alyssa.

"Will you shut up?" she yelled back. "You screamed so loud before, I thought the whole neighborhood was going to wake up."

Next door, Mrs. Watson was sleeping soundly, having

finally escaped from the dream of that unpleasant concert. For the last half-hour, Minnie, one of Mrs. Watson's three cats, was peering out the window into Sean's bedroom. The pudgy calico turned repeatedly with a soft meow, reporting on the strange things happening across the way.

Minnie could see the mean boy, who always chased her. He was flapping his arms at the nice girl, who sometimes scratched Minnie's triangular ears.

"We have to tell someone!"

"That's the fourth time you've said that," snarled Alyssa, collecting her thoughts.

"Come back, Buddies," said Sean, staring at the mirror. The small stars pulsed stronger, beckoning him forward. Sean pressed his body against the drawers.

"Everyone be quiet," ordered Alyssa. "Let's try to figure out what is happening."

"What is happening is that we should call the police," said Bradley, beginning to pace. "We have ghosts in our house. I mean, we should do something. We should tell someone."

Alyssa raised her hand and stroked the wand's cool glass across her cheek. Annie named it the Essence. *The essence of what?*

"We really should call Mom and Dad," she said.

"Mom and Dad? They're like hours away," said Bradley. "We have to dial 9-1-1. This is an emergency."

"9-1-1? And report what? That ghosts are in our house. We need to call Mom and Dad."

The debate continued without regard for the growing danger. Alyssa argued for speaking to their parents. Bradley argued for calling the police. And Sean began climbing up the dresser in search of the Buddies.

With her finger pointed at Bradley, Alyssa turned her head, spotting the bottom of Sean's pajamas and his small, bare feet sticking out of the mirror. Before she could open her mouth, he was gone.

In Mrs. Watson's bedroom, Minnie yawned, but maintained her watch. The mean boy yelled a lot tonight. But now the nice girl was screaming.

Chapter 6
Into the Mirror

The screaming went on for quite a while, ending with Alyssa and Bradley futilely shouting their brother's name at the mirror. Alyssa's knees buckled. Fearful of collapsing, she wobbled over to Sean's bed. Burying her head, she moaned the words, "I have to think," over and over into the blanket, while Bradley paced around the room mumbling, "Mom and Dad are going to kill us. They are going to kill us."

The mirror continued sparkling without a reflection. Stopping in front of it, Bradley dipped his head toward the surface, listening for his brother's voice, Annie's voice, Benny's voice, or anyone's voice.

"What are you doing?" shouted Alyssa. "Get away from there."

"Shhh," responded Bradley, thrusting his hand back to quiet his sister. "I think I hear something."

Alyssa jumped off the bed to join him. Heads together, they both listened intently. Bradley momentarily heard a faint, unintelligible whisper. He looked at his sister. *I heard it too*, she thought. But after a silent minute passed, Alyssa set aside her fears and resolved to take action.

"I have to get him," she said, standing up.

Bradley's eyes widened. "Get him? You mean go in and get him?"

Alyssa stared at the shimmering entrance. *An entrance to what*, she wondered. "Yes. I mean go in and get him."

"You're not leaving me here by myself," said Bradley, crossing his arms. "You're the one in charge. You should have been watching him. This is your fault."

Alyssa growled and shoved her brother. Bradley stumbled backward, regained his balance, and lashed out with a fist, striking his sister's left arm. Her face flushed, Alyssa shook with rage and readied herself for a full assault. Bradley crouched down and prepared to defend himself. They stood rigid, staring at each other, until finally Alyssa's eyes welled up.

What am I doing? she thought, coming to her senses. *I have to get Sean.*

Bradley watched his sister and relaxed. An idea popped into his brain. "What if you tie a rope around me? I'll go in and when I have Sean, I'll tug on the rope and you can pull us out."

"I don't know," said Alyssa, tears trickling down her ashen cheeks. "We don't even know what's in there."

"Look, this is hard for me to admit, but you're right," said Bradley, gagging on the last word. "We have to get Sean. And either we wait until he comes back out, or we go in and get him. With a rope around me at least you can pull us through, if we can't find our way back."

"That's if you find him. We don't even know what's in there," repeated Alyssa forcefully.

"I know but . . . but we know Sean's in there. We have to try."

Alyssa's stomach churned. What was she doing? All she imagined was more tragedy awaiting her. Alyssa pictured her parents arriving home Sunday afternoon, finding her alone at a kitchen table covered with stacks of moldy pancakes.

What then? *I should have called Mom and Dad when I had the chance.*

"Okay," she said weakly. "But you're not going through. I am."

"No way," countered Bradley.

"Yes way."

"No way," he repeated. "If there's a problem, I won't be able to pull you out. You weigh a ton more than me."

Alyssa gritted her teeth. "I do not weigh a ton more than you."

Bradley ignored her and dashed out of the room. "Where are you going?" yelled Alyssa.

"To get a rope!"

The Dempsey basement was a fairly typical family dumping ground. The regularly-used materials – fans, cases of canned soda, boxes of pasta purchased in quantity, and board games – were organized in an accessible corner by the stairs. The barely-touched items – Bradley's old tricycle, a slide projector screen, a collection of tools their father rarely used, and the camping equipment – were piled in the back, serving little purpose other than accumulating thick, grey dust.

Bradley waded through the mess and cobwebs to the camping gear. His father hiked and backpacked with him before Sean was born, but not since. "The house is too busy now that we have three," his father said. The explanation was another reason for Bradley to resent his little brother.

He began to search for the long, thin, red ropes his father used to tie down their tent when the skies darkened. "Anything stays down in the wind and rain if the rope is strong enough," his father taught him.

Bradley moved aside a tattered, sea-blue tarp, exposing a small, black spider. He jumped back while the spider retreated for quieter quarters. Pushing boxes aside, Bradley created a sour, murky dust cloud, generating three strong sneezes. Finally, after a few minutes of searching, he found an unopened, white box generically labeled, "Nylon Rope – 100 Feet."

From upstairs, Alyssa's muffled cry carried through two floors. "Hurry!"

Bounding up both flights of steps, Bradley stopped in his room to reclaim his *Hero Warrior* sword before returning to Sean's bedroom.

"Will you put that thing down?" demanded his sister.

Bradley raised the beaded, plastic weapon to his chest. "I'm the one going in there, so I'm taking it."

Alyssa shook her head. At this point, finding Sean was her primary concern. She removed the weather-faded red rope from the box and began threading it through the belt loops on Bradley's shorts. He carefully tied a slip-knot.

"Plaid shorts and a plastic sword," remarked Alyssa. "If there are other ghosts in there, please don't mention that we're related."

"Should I wear baggy sweatpants like you to hide my fat butt?"

With a scowl, Alyssa pinched Bradley quite hard. Angrily eyeing each other, brother and sister tugged the rope, testing the knot. It was firm. Alyssa's shoulders dropped and she tentatively touched Bradley's hand.

"Just get him," she whispered.

Alyssa put the Essence on the floor and grabbed the rope, while Bradley hoisted himself on to the wooden dresser. Alyssa held up her left hand and spread her fingers.

"Five minutes. If you are not out by then I'm pulling you out."

Bradley nodded. Half-closing his eyes, he reached

forward and touched the mirror's glistening surface, letting the tips of his fingers push in.

"It feels like wet jelly," he reported.

The face of the mirror was undisturbed. It remained textured, full of tiny, white stars. *There are thousands of them.* Bradley pulled out his hand and shook it. Nothing dripped off. *It's dry,* he thought, wiggling his fingers at his sister.

"I'll tug on the rope," he said, looking one last time at Alyssa.

"Be careful," she replied.

Gathering his courage with a deep breath, as well as for oxygen should none exist where he was going, Bradley closed his eyes, sinking through the barrier between Sean's bedroom and the black unknown. Alyssa watched helplessly as another brother for whom she was responsible disappeared from her sight.

She held the rope tautly, feeding a few inches at a time as her brother moved unseen on the other side. They agreed on five minutes and Alyssa began counting when Bradley disappeared.

"24, 25, 26 . . ."

Please, she thought. *Please let Sean be okay.*

"37, 38 . . ."

I'll do anything. I'll go to church more. I'll be nicer to Bradley.

"52, 53 . . ."

I'll give my allowance to charity. I'll help Mrs. Watson take in her grocery bags.

"73, 74 . . ."

Alyssa suddenly realized she never calculated how many seconds were in five minutes. *Sixty seconds in a minute. Sixty times five was –*

Benny burst through the mirror's surface. Floating in the air, his face pressed close with obvious concern. Startled by the ghost's unexpected appearance, Alyssa lost her grip on the rope and it slipped forwarded. She tightened her hands and felt the nylon stinging her palms.

"Pull him back," Benny shouted.

"What?" asked Alyssa, trying to remember the last number of her count.

"Pull him back," repeated Benny frantically.

Alyssa held the rope firmly. "Does he have Sean? Does he have my little brother?"

"It doesn't matter," said Benny. "We have to close it."

"Close what?"

"The mirror," he responded anxiously, pointing at the sparkling portal. "We have to close the mirror."

No, thought Alyssa. She did not care about pancakes. Or bicycles. Or the Buddies. Or the Essence. Or the mirror.

"No," she shouted, refusing to part with the red rope, snaking slowly through her hands. "Not without my brothers!"

"It's not safe," pleaded Benny. "Annie has to close it."

Alyssa turned and saw the fear in Benny's white, puffy face. The rope shuddered in her hands and stopped moving. *Something is wrong.* Alyssa's heart sank. *I have to pull Bradley out.*

Squeezing her hands on the line linking her with Bradley, Alyssa heaved backward without success. She tugged harder, eyes fixed on the tiny dots of light slowly fading beneath the face of the mirror. The star-points drifted to the center, silently submerged, and disappeared. The glass reformed from the outer edges of the white oak frame, rushing inwards and swiftly slicing the red, nylon rope, like a sharp pair of scissors cutting paper. Falling backward, Alyssa saw her astonished reflection reappear.

No, she thought, scrambling to her feet. *No!*

There was Alyssa. Messy, brown hair. Coffee ice-cream stained, white t-shirt. Grey sweats. And a big ghost floating by her side, both of them gawking at their reflections in the restored glass.

Benny searched for something helpful to say, but instead he stated the obvious.

"This is not a good thing."

The Essence
Book II
Saturday
and the
Nothing
Vel Grande
Illustrations by Krystle Carkeek

"I'd give you all of my dreams,
if you'd help me find a door
that doesn't lead me back again."

Genesis, *The Chamber of 32 Doors*

Chapter 1
Breakfast with Benny

It was a rather atypical breakfast. To begin with, one of the two diners, a portly gentleman named Benny, was dead. It was a long time since Benny last ate and, as a ghost, there was no possibility of him sharing a meal that morning with his female companion.

Unlike Benny, the young lady was alive. She could eat as much or as little as she desired. Her name was Alyssa Dempsey, and she sat staring blankly at hundreds of cold, stale pancakes stacked in large piles on the dark-brown walnut kitchen table of her family's home. Unfortunately, and not surprisingly, on this particular Saturday morning Alyssa was not hungry for stale pancakes, fresh pancakes, or anything else.

Before her parents left for their twentieth wedding anniversary weekend, they assigned Alyssa the task of caring for her two younger brothers, Bradley and Sean. Less than twenty-four hours after her parents' departure, both brothers disappeared into a mirror inhabited by ghosts. This sad situation was the understandable cause of Alyssa's lack of appetite.

For the moment, Benny was oblivious to Alyssa's predicament, which he referred to as a "terrible pickle" when they finally gave up their vigil in front of the solid-glass mirror in Sean's bedroom. Benny was busy floating around the kitchen, sticking his head through the refrigerator, pantry, and cabinet doors.

"I love food," he said for the fifth time. "I wish I could eat again. Everything looks so yummy."

Drifting along the edge of the kitchen counter, Benny noticed wilted flowers by the sink, lying in plastic wrap, where Alyssa left them before Sean began his wishing spree for pancakes the previous morning. Alyssa's boyfriend Will brought her the beautiful bouquet before visiting his grandparents for the weekend. When she received them, their fresh, aromatic smell and bright colors filled her head. But now the white flowers were turning yellow, the yellow ones were turning orange, and the orange flowers were brown. And Will was far away.

"You should put these in water," remarked Benny. "They don't look so great."

"Would you please be quiet?" asked Alyssa, fighting back tears.

Benny empathized with her plight. He stood with Alyssa for over two hours in front of Sean's mirror, doing his best to comfort her after it closed, trapping her brothers in his world and Benny in the Dempsey home. At dawn he announced that the mirror would not open until the evening, whereupon the unlikely pair made their way to the first floor, Alyssa walking down the steps with Benny floating behind her.

As Alyssa sat dejectedly at the kitchen table, Benny tried a couple of silly jokes and funny faces to cheer her up, until she looked at him crossly and said, "I'm not a baby. Leave me alone."

Benny missed the fragrant smell of fresh-cut flowers and thought it was a shame to let them dry up and die. He missed the taste of food. He missed the warmth of hugs.

"Your brothers are going to be all right," Benny said gently. "Annie is really smart."

Alyssa opened her mouth to respond, but something in the Dempsey's backyard and garden caught Benny's attention as he peered through their large kitchen window.

"Squirrels," he shouted gleefully. "And birds. I love birds!"

"Where are they?" asked Alyssa.

"Right there in the trees," said Benny, pointing with a white, misty finger. "I hope I see cardinals. They're so pretty."

"Not the birds," barked Alyssa. "Where are my brothers?"

Benny turned to her. "They're in the Nothing," he said gravely.

"The Nothing?"

"The Nothing," repeated Benny with a sigh. "Sometimes

when you die, you go back to another life right away. You become a whole new person starting as a baby all over again without remembering who you were before. But usually you go to the Nothing and wait for a new life. Maybe you wait a short time. Or maybe you wait a long time. It's not predictable."

Alyssa thought of her brothers in a place for the dead, surrounded by creepy ghosts. *Can you see in there?* she wondered. *Can you breathe?* Her mind raced with questions and she fired them at Benny, who tried his best to respond.

"I don't know what it's like to be alive in the Nothing. But Annie would never hurt your brothers, so I think they're okay."

"You think?" Alyssa complained. "They better be okay or I'm going to kill you."

Benny smiled sadly and said, "Too late for that." Alyssa wanted to laugh. Benny was funny and she liked him, but wanting to laugh was not enough. Instead, Alyssa lowered her head, sinking back into despair.

"Is Annie your wife?" she asked.

"I wish!" exclaimed Benny. "No. She's too beautiful and too smart to marry someone like me. I had a nice wife. I'm sure she's alive. We should go visit her," he added in a mischievous tone.

The corners of Alyssa's lips turned up slightly. "I don't think that's a good idea."

"Probably not," Benny agreed. "Do you have a boyfriend?"

"Yes," replied Alyssa absently. She thought of Will's smile and longed for his tall frame and comforting hug. Feeling the sadness rise, Alyssa pressed for more information. "Do you remember your old life?"

"Sure," said Benny, sporting a pale, white grin. "I was

a mailman. I really liked delivering mail. Even through rain and sleet and snow. I met so many nice people." He paused for a moment. "I guess I still deliver things. I delivered the Essence to Sean."

"Why do you call it the Essence?" asked Alyssa, remembering the cause of her misery. She gazed at Sean's glass wishing wand. Red liquid waves rolled through its center. Alyssa silently wished that her brothers were home. Nothing happened. Only Sean created what he wanted with the wand.

Benny turned back to the sun-filled window. "I wonder if I'll see a chipmunk. I really like chipmunks," he said without answering Alyssa's question. Benny's eyes lingered on the Dempsey backyard, but they flicked to the side, tinted with guilt.

Alyssa stood and confronted the ghost. "Why do you call it the Essence?"

Benny sighed and his snowy face grew a shade darker. "When I first came to the Nothing, there were a lot of people who were dead for a really long time. They were confused why they were there so long, and they wanted to find a way out, to get to a new life. Around the same time I died, there were also twin brothers with me in the Nothing. They made the Essence as a way to escape."

As Benny spoke, the wand warmed in Alyssa's hand. Inside the glass, a small, crimson storm raged, responding to the ghost's words.

"I'm not exactly sure how they made it, but that's what they called it," he continued. "The Essence. But after it was made one brother kept it for himself and the other disappeared. And the brother who had the Essence used it to keep all of us in the Nothing. Annie, me, and everyone else who wants to be alive again. We can't leave. We can't live a new life."

"Why?" asked Alyssa.

"Why do all bad people do mean things?" Benny answered flatly. Alyssa shrugged. "It gives them power. He likes being the boss. He likes it more than being alive again."

Alyssa raised the wand. The shiny, red liquid rushed back and forth, expanding at each end. A large bubble shaped like a man's face momentarily appeared.

"That's him," said Benny.

"Him?" Alyssa jumped and the Essence nearly slipped from her hand. "He's inside of here?"

"Not really," replied Benny. "Part of him, I think. I'm not sure."

Annoyed, Alyssa wondered if Benny really was clueless, or whether he was hiding information from her. *Information I need to help find my brothers*, she thought.

"How is the one brother still keeping everyone in the Nothing without this Essence?" she asked, waving the wand at him.

Hesitant, Benny sucked his dry, puffy lips. "That's a good question. I think as long as it exists, we're stuck."

"Well, we have the Essence!" Alyssa shouted excitedly. "If this bad guy is in there we can just destroy it. We can destroy him!"

Benny shook his head. "No. Annie says it can't be destroyed. At least not by us. It has to be kept safe." The ghost's voice trailed off and Alyssa was certain he was concealing something. Benny changed the subject. "Can you make breakfast now, so I can pretend to eat?"

Tightening her grip, Alyssa smashed the wand down on the edge of the wooden kitchen table. The violent impact shook the stacks of cold pancakes and echoed loudly through the Dempsey house. Alyssa's arm stung terribly from the force of the blow. She examined her hand, expecting blood and shards of glass embedded in her palm.

Nothing, she thought, amazed. The Essence was undamaged. *I didn't even chip it.*

Benny chuckled softly. "I told you."

Once more Alyssa lifted the wand, this time grasping it with two determined hands and whipping the glass against the table. Pain erupted in her wrists, slicing up her arms and ending with a cry from her mouth. She collapsed, her knees striking the ceramic floor. She could feel the unbroken glass facets pressing on her fingers. Her eyes, level with the table, saw a small, jagged crack in the deep-brown walnut at the point of impact.

Another thing I messed up, thought Alyssa. Defeat flooded her throbbing arms.

"I told you," Benny said sympathetically. "Annie says it can't be destroyed."

Maybe he's telling the truth. Alyssa did not know. She crawled to her feet, and then fell back into the kitchen chair, dropping the Essence on her lap. "I'm so tired," she said, sighing.

"I wish I could be tired," Benny replied. "I haven't slept in years."

Years, wondered Alyssa. *How could you be awake for years?* Her head swam with questions again. "What is the bad brother's name?"

"Patrick," Benny replied bitterly.

"Does he make pancakes with the Essence, too?" she joked.

"No," the ghost said flatly. "Patrick is bad and he makes bad things so he can be the boss. Creatures. That's why we checked on your brother last night."

Alyssa's heart fell to her feet. "Creatures," she whispered, hoping she misheard him.

"Yes," replied Benny, nodding. "We have to be careful. Tonight he might send creatures through the mirror and try to take the Essence back."

He shook his cloudy-white head and smiled. "Are you ready to make breakfast?"

Chapter 2
The Nothing

Passing through Sean's mirror, Bradley Dempsey trudged blindly through what felt like an unending black wall of dense water. The red nylon rope, looped through his shorts, remained tight, providing his only source of comfort, that his sister Alyssa was connected to him in case he was lucky enough to find Sean in this dark, thick world.

Bradley grasped the plastic handle of his *Hero Warrior* sword with both hands, slowly waving it from side to side, desperately searching for something of substance. Off to his right, he heard noises that eventually sounded like words, as if someone was speaking another language.

He opened his mouth, trying to call Sean's name. Nothing emerged. *I'm not breathing,* Bradley thought. He had taken a deep breath before penetrating the mirror's surface. *That was my last one,* he recalled, while fishing in the darkness with his sword. *Am I dead?*

An empty taste filled Bradley's mouth, similar to chewing on paper. A lifeless smell of dusty wood slithered into his nose. More indecipherable words were spoken, this time to Bradley's left. And then again to his right. A conversation was ongoing, but between whom?

The material around him fluttered, and Bradley felt someone or something rush past his side, heading back toward the mirror. Waterless waves pushed at Bradley in the wake of the movement, and he turned around, hoping to see what was happening. The rope slackened and he lurched forward. Clutching his sword, Bradley reached for the lifeline with his free hand, but in vain. The rope was gone.

"Alyssa," he shouted, whipping his body around in the dark. "Help! Help me!"

"Open your eyes."

Bradley stopped moving and tilted his head, listening. He was certain he heard someone say –

"Open your eyes," the voice repeated. It was a man's voice, calm but firm and very close. The man sounded like –

"Dad?"

"No," said the man. "I'm not your father. Go ahead and open your eyes."

Confused, Bradley flailed about with his sword. He searched the darkness. Nothing was there except the voice. "They're open," he said.

"No, they are not," continued the man. "Imagine them open."

Imagine them open, thought Bradley. *What does that mean?*

He pretended his eyes were open and, unexpectedly, they filled with a soft, faint light. A man and a woman stood in front of him. Not ghosts. A real man and a real woman, dressed in seamless white clothes that flowed over their bodies. Bradley focused on the woman's human face. It was Annie. Her eyes, shaded black by the darkness, glared angrily at him.

"How could you do such a foolish thing?" Annie demanded sternly.

Why am I the bad guy? Bradley thought resentfully. It was their fault for opening the mirror and letting Sean through.

“Where’s my brother?” asked Bradley, pointing his finger at her.

My finger? Bradley’s finger was a long, thin, white cloud. *My hand*, he thought, counting four milky fingers and a matching thumb. *My hands! My arms! My feet!*

Bradley’s pale, translucent figure swirled around. But wherever Bradley looked, he found nothing solid, only the same sheer silhouette that Annie and Benny looked like in Sean’s room. Even his plastic *Hero Warrior* sword was a shimmering, wispy blade. *I’m a ghost!*

"What happened?" he shouted. "What's wrong with me? Am I dead?"

The man calmly stepped forward. Once again, Bradley thought of his father. The man was definitely a grownup, but still young, about the same age as Annie. *Maybe twenty or thirty,* thought Bradley. He wasn't sure. The man's full, brown hair was brushed back in thick lines, capping a serious but welcoming square-shaped face. He was not chubby, like Benny. This was someone different.

"You are not dead," the man said. "In our world you are a spirit, just as you saw Annie and Benny when they were spirits in your world. When you return, you will be yourself again."

The man smiled reassuringly. "And so will your toy sword," he added.

Bradley fired off questions without waiting for answers. "What is this place? How do I get back? Where's Sean? Where's Benny?"

"This place is the Nothing," replied the man, "where people wait for another life after they die. Annie and I closed the mirror, which is a doorway between the Nothing and your brother's room. Benny is with your sister."

"I want to go back," interrupted Bradley. "I want Sean and I want to go back right now!"

"Be quiet!" shouted Annie. "He's trying to talk to you."

Startled by her outburst, Bradley floated backward a few inches. The man gazed at Annie, his lips slightly curling up at the ends. "We just don't have a lot of time," she said, apologizing.

He turned back to Bradley. "We closed the mirror because right now it's not safe. There are things in this place that want the wand Annie and Benny gave to your brother. Mean things," he emphasized. "Annie tells me your sister has the wand, which we call the Essence. The mean things will try to go through the mirror to take it from your sister."

I don't buy it, Bradley thought. Raising the sword and pointing his other ghost arm at Annie, he said, "Then why did you give the stupid wishing wand to Sean? And where is my brother? I'm getting him and I'm going home."

Annie growled. "You impetuous –"

The man lifted a hand, quieting Annie before she launched another verbal assault. Recognizing the boy's anxiety, he approached Bradley slowly.

"Everything's going to be okay." Bradley's sword tipped down. His father always said that when Bradley was upset. "I'll look for Sean now," continued the man. "You wait here with Annie."

"What?" cried Bradley. "I'm not staying here with her. She's worse than my sister!"

The man ignored him and turned to Annie. "Are you ready?"

Bradley watched as she nodded silently, mixed with fear and sadness. "Be careful," she said quietly.

What is going on? he wondered. But before Bradley voiced any further displeasure or concern, the man turned and ran off into the blackness. For a short time, Bradley could see his white clothes in the distance, until the man became a fading dot, finally disappearing into the unending night.

Left by themselves in the Nothing, Bradley and Annie made an odd, unhappy couple. She gave him a silent, sharp warning not to bother her. Annie nervously scanned the mysterious darkness surrounding them for any sign of danger.

While they waited, Bradley experimented, moving the ghost limbs that replaced his arms and legs. With a little practice he was able to spin around. Behind him, Bradley discovered a large, black rectangle standing on its short side with a glowing, light-blue border. It reminded him of the neon signs on the boardwalk when his family vacationed at the beach, except in the middle there were no words like PIZZA, or FUDGE, or –

"Ice cream," Bradley said softly. He wondered whether there was food in the Nothing.

"What?" asked Annie.

Floating, Bradley spun around and faced her. "Is that the mirror in Sean's room?" he asked, pointing the sword back at the rectangle.

"Yes," she replied blandly, continuing her watch. "And put that sword down."

"And put that sword down," mimicked Bradley. *She's just like my sister.*

Bored, Bradley the ghost hovered around, occasionally peeking at Annie's real face. He liked her hair, which fell across her cheek, slipping past one eye and her thin nose. She's sort of pretty. Embarrassed, he immediately squelched the thought. When seventh grade started, Bradley began noticing how girls looked, and it annoyed him. Worse, girls talked to him more. Last week, Miranda Stevens asked him to have lunch with her. Of course, he refused.

Bradley cleared his mind. "It looks open to me." He waited for Annie's response. "Is it open?"

"It's closed," said Annie. "It's just a marker. The entire door would be lit blue if it was open." Annie crossed her arms. "No more questions, please. I'm busy."

"You don't look busy to me," snapped Bradley. He stared back at the door to Sean's mirror and for a moment considered trying to go through.

Maybe she's lying to me, he wondered. *But I can't go*

back without Sean. Alyssa will kill me. Annie twisted her head, searching the Nothing. *Alyssa's lucky. At least she has Benny. That's a lot better than hanging with anxious Annie.*

Bradley practiced moving, keeping himself occupied in the Nothing. The man was right. Testing his ghost body, Bradley found he could float in any direction by imagining the action. *Up*, he thought, and he lifted away from the black surface where Annie stood. He even flipped upside-down. *This is cool!*

"Well? What do you think?" asked an inverted Bradley, smiling at Annie and fishing for a compliment. "Pretty awesome!"

She rolled her eyes, but offered no praise. When she looked away, Bradley stuck out his white tongue.

He rolled back over and looked into the Nothing. *This place is really black*, he thought. In every direction it seemed like someone had layered dark, sheer curtains. Bradley could see Annie, but searching around he found no source of light illuminating her face, her hair, and the white clothes flowing down her body. He examined his hands and sword, stretching them out in the darkness. They shimmered softly.

We make the light, he thought. *That's why I could see the man when he ran off. His clothes and body were glowing.*

"Who is he?" asked Bradley.

"Who is who?" replied Annie.

"The man just here who's looking for Sean! He looked familiar. Or at least he sounded familiar, anyway. Who is he?"

Annie shifted her body uncomfortably. "A friend. That's all you need to know."

"Your friend? Benny's friend?" Annie remained silent. "Is he a ghost like you?"

Annoyed, she glared at Bradley. "Tell me!" he shouted, spinning around her.

"Will you stop that?" demanded Annie.

"But this is fun," cried Bradley, moving in faster circles and watching Annie's temper rise. *She's just like Alyssa. I will never like girls*, he thought, soaring through the Nothing. *They are so mean!*

Annie stuck her right hand into Bradley's flight path. He smiled triumphantly, defiantly raising his *Hero Warrior* sword. "I'm a ghost. You can't stop me!"

But Bradley never said "me." Instead, at the word "stop" he slammed into Annie's outstretched hand, tumbling down to her feet. Dazed, he shook his misty, cloud-colored head.

A victorious Annie smirked.

"You are no ghost," she said, whipping her index finger. "And this is not a playground. Did you hear what he said? There are dangerous things here."

"He said mean things. He probably said that to make me listen to you," Bradley replied, pouting. "Well, I'm not listening to you until you tell me who he is!"

A hideously loud scream arose from the black Nothing. The scream's intense volume and evil pitch raised Bradley's ghost-hair. Frightened, he sought Annie's face, and found tight, ashen lips and dark, inky eyes filled with concern.

"Okay," said Bradley. "I'm listening now."

Chapter 3
The Phone Call

As the afternoon wore on, Alyssa felt less and less like talking. Benny left her alone, happily exploring his new surroundings. She watched as he passed effortlessly through walls, ceilings and floors, until Alyssa tired of his running commentary about the construction of their home. Exhausted, she sank into the family room sofa and fell asleep.

The doorbell rang at three o'clock, startling Alyssa. She leapt down the hall, hoping Will returned early from visiting his grandparents. Alyssa swung the front door open, revealing old Mrs. Watson, standing in the entryway and dressed in a blue, floral housecoat with a wild shock of grey hair ranging in mixed patterns. Mrs. Watson announced that her three cats were fixated on the Dempsey residence, immovable from her windows facing their home.

"They won't even come for their favorite treats," the elderly woman complained. "Is something strange going on in here?"

Alyssa's heart pounded, but she kept her cool and said, "My brothers were a little noisy earlier. I'll tell them to keep it down." Realizing she held the Essence, Alyssa quickly tucked the glass wand behind her back.

Dissatisfied with the girl's explanation, Mrs. Watson said, "Well, if this keeps up I'll be speaking with your parents."

If this keeps up, thought Alyssa, *I'll be hiding from my parents.*

After the old woman tromped off without a goodbye, Alyssa shut the door and returned to the family room to discover Benny on the sofa reading *Charlotte's Web*. The book hovered in the air in front him. As he read, the pages turned by themselves.

"That's just creepy," said Alyssa.

Benny let the comment pass. "This is a great story. Did you ever read it?"

"Sort of," she replied. "My mom read it to me. How do you do that?"

"Do what?" Benny asked. Alyssa pointed at the book floating in front of the big ghost. "You have to imagine it," he explained.

"Imagine it? Just because you imagine something doesn't mean it can happen," stated Alyssa, although after yesterday she was unsure of what she believed.

"That's how it works for me," said Benny, smiling. "That's how it works in the Nothing."

"But you aren't in the Nothing," Alyssa stated.

Benny sighed. "True."

Expecting more, Alyssa waited. But Benny returned to his book and continued reading. She impatiently tapped the Essence on her leg. Benny's habit of offering incomplete answers felt intentional.

"What's your boyfriend's name?" he asked without looking at her.

"His name is Will. And you are doing that a lot," said Alyssa.

"Doing what?"

"Changing the subject," she retorted, clenching her teeth. Another page turned by itself and Alyssa lost her temper. She raced around the couch and snapped the book out of the air. "Listen, you ghoul! I want answers. Both of my brothers are trapped in your Nothing and I want answers!"

Benny flashed a supportive grin. "It's not my Nothing, but what do you want to know?"

Alyssa's mind went blank. Her anger faded, replaced by fear. And she hated questions when she was afraid. It was worse than solving a math word problem. *If two brothers disappear into the Nothing on Friday night and never return, what time on Sunday afternoon before my parents get back should I run away?*

"What do you want to know?" repeated Benny.

"It's been a long time since Sean and Bradley got stuck on the other side of the mirror. How do you know they're okay?" asked Alyssa.

"Actually, your brothers haven't been gone for a long time, because time is different in the Nothing. It's slower," explained Benny.

"Slower?"

"Yes. Slower. Which makes us faster. At least I think that's how it works." Benny's pale eyes drifted up, as he reconsidered what he said. "Yep. Definitely slower."

Alyssa waited for more while Benny silently mouthed some calculations, confirming his answer on the time question. "How do you know they are okay?" she repeated forcefully.

"Hmm? Oh. Actually, I don't. But they're with Annie and, like I said, she's pretty smart. She's the one who stole the Essence."

The teenage girl's blue eyes widened. "She stole it from Patrick?" Benny nodded. "How did she steal it?"

The ghost hesitated. "I don't know."

Alyssa stamped her feet on the carpet in frustration. "Stop that! You do know! You're worse than Bradley."

Recalling her mother's advice about her brother, Alyssa closed her eyes, inhaled deeply, and slowly counted out loud from ten to zero. Amused, Benny tapped his white fingers on his full, chalky face.

"I still don't know," he said compassionately, when she finished.

"I guess Annie imagined it," Alyssa replied sarcastically.

More questions flashed in her head. Why did Annie and Benny give the Essence to Sean? Why could Sean make wishes with it and no one else?

"Why Sean?"

Benny did not know. Maybe Annie knew.

"You're not very helpful," complained Alyssa. "I should've been stuck here with Annie. Then maybe I'd have some answers."

A sad shadow passed across Benny's round face, and silence filled the family room. Dejected, Benny looked away. "I guess I'm not a big help."

"I'm sorry," said Alyssa, tasting cold, sour regret on her tongue. "I'm sorry I said that."

She dropped on the couch next to Benny, and stared momentarily into the oval mirror hung on the other side of the family room. Seeing the reflection of the plump ghost seated next to her reminded Alyssa of the Haunted Mansion at Disney World. She was twelve when her parents took her and Bradley. Pregnant with Sean, her mom and Alyssa shared an egg-shaped "Doom Buggy" while the young girl gazed at a mirror on the ride's wall, reflecting a freaky, bright-green ghoul between them. But when Alyssa searched inside their canopied car, there was no ghost, only her mom's round belly.

Alyssa needed to ask Benny the nagging, frightening question that was on her mind ever since he said the word at breakfast. Creatures.

Alyssa swallowed. "What about the creatures? You said creatures might come through the mirror and try to take the Essence back." Benny nodded at her. "Do you mean monsters?"

"Lost Souls," he moaned. "Lost Souls protect Patrick. They were people like you and me, but they have no next life and they're really nasty. And if they touch you, then you won't have a next life, either." Benny paused. "Or maybe it's just if they touch dead people like me. It may not work if they touch a living person. You might be okay. Hmmm," he murmured with his voice trailing off.

Alyssa waited patiently for more. Finally, Benny turned to her. "Do you want to watch cartoons?"

Burying her head in her hands, Alyssa heard the television turn on. Her cheeks flushed while the sounds of animated chaos filled the room. "I love cartoons," announced the ghost.

Alyssa's anger flashed, but salvation arrived for Benny as the Dempseys' telephone rang, piercing the air from the kitchen. The teenage girl's head twisted, her long hair flying through Benny's misty face.

"Call from Dempsey Less-Lee," announced a micro-chip generated electronic voice, after a second shrill ring. Trying to grab Benny's shoulder, Alyssa's hand shot into his body.

"Oh my God! It's my mom! What am I going to say?"

"Do you want me to talk to her?" asked Benny, as the third ring ended.

"No!"

Benny shrugged as Alyssa raced from the couch, picking up the phone before the answering machine engaged.

"Hello," said Alyssa, her voice cracking. "Hi . . . no. I just didn't know where the phone was. Okay . . . really everything's okay . . . they're being good . . . no . . . they're outside in the backyard playing . . . yeah, really . . . are you having a good time?"

A huge laugh burst from Benny's mouth. Alyssa froze, realizing her mom heard him.

"What . . . oh that . . . that was just my friend . . . well he's actually a friend of Will's . . . who . . . umm . . . Benny . . . Benny who?"

Alyssa covered the phone and shouted "What's your last name?"

Watching the television, Benny chuckled and turned. "Evechikowski."

Alyssa glared at him. "Really!" she barked, annoyed.

"Benny Smith," she lied. "Yes . . . yes . . . what . . . no he's not a new boyfriend." Benny rolled his eyes excitedly. "Shut up," yelled Alyssa at him, covering the phone again.

"What?" she asked, returning to her mother. The rosy color of Alyssa's cheeks drained away. "What time tomorrow? . . . maybe if you're having fun you should stay longer . . . you can. It's okay. I can watch them."

Hearing her desperation, Benny rose and drifted to Alyssa. As he approached the kitchen, her shoulders slumped forward, draped by tangled, brown hair.

"Okay . . . okay . . . thanks . . . I love you too." Alyssa tossed the phone aside. It landed softly on a pile of cold chocolate-chip pancakes. An uncertain stillness hung between the ghost and the girl.

"She said she was proud of me," murmured Alyssa, breaking the silence.

"Do you want to talk?" asked Benny.

Alyssa shook her head. "I need to go to my bed," she replied sadly. Benny watched the sullen teenager shuffle down the hall, turning to climb the stairs. *Oh well*, he thought, *back to cartoons.*

In her room, crawling under the covers, Alyssa clutched the Essence to her chest as she stared at the ceiling. *I'm the worst sister ever*, she thought. *How could I let Sean go through the mirror? How did I let Bradley follow him with our stupid plan?*

Alyssa's cell phone beeped, letting her know she received a text message. Will's words blared in capitalized, block text.

LONGTIME NO HEAR. WHY SO QUIET? EVERYTHING OKAY? I LOVE YOU.

Alyssa started a reply, typing a few letters. *What should I write*, she thought. *I can't take care of his worrying. I can't take care of anything.*

Throwing her phone on the nightstand, Alyssa closed her eyes and drifted into a heavy, dreamless slumber.

* * *

Hours later, a loud thump popped out of Sean's room, across the hall. Cocooned tightly in her blanket, Alyssa's eyes snapped open.

"Watch it, you idiot," whispered an angry voice.

"Don't tell me what to do," replied another.

Oh no, thought Alyssa. *Lost Souls*.

Chapter 4
The Shriek

Another terrible scream sliced across the stagnant Nothing. Dimly lit outlines of other figures abruptly appeared, scurrying away from the horrible sound's unseen source, and all moving toward Annie and Bradley.

"Follow me," ordered Annie, turning swiftly and breaking into a run. Bradley floated alongside her, peering back with fearful curiosity. The light-blue rectangle's glow, marking the mirror in Sean's room, faded in the retreating, black haze.

"What is it?" asked Bradley.

From his right, a short, grey-haired, old man dressed in seamless white, like Annie, crossed their path, whimpering while sprinting past them. "Run," he said urgently, and then disappeared into the darkness.

Old people are fast here, thought Bradley. Others were visible, rapidly distancing themselves from the screaming. None interacted with them.

"What is it?" he repeated.

Another gruesome shrill, higher pitched and longer than the previous cries, quickened the pace of everyone hurrying through the Nothing. Except Annie, who suddenly stopped.

Bradley floated past her, and then swiveled his pasty body. Annie remained motionless with her head down, waiting for the next scream. “Why are we stopping?” he asked forcefully.

Annie threw up a hand to silence him, and tilted her head, listening intently. Bradley spun anxiously, expecting the monster making the noises to appear out of the never-ending night. *I hate this place*, he thought. *Hate it, hate it, hate it!*

“Follow me,” said Annie, and she began jogging slowly.

“Are you going to tell me what that is?” shouted Bradley over another horrible blast.

Annie stopped, again. “That was quieter,” she murmured softly.

"Quieter! It sounded pretty loud to me!" yelled Bradley, clutching his sword defensively. *She's wacko,* he thought, staring at her. Annie remained frozen, listening intently as one more scream pierced the Nothing's oppressive film.

"Shhh," she whispered, anticipating another question from the teenage boy. The hideous voice let loose and Bradley silently agreed that it was a little quieter than the previous scream.

"We're faster than it," he said excitedly. "Let's keep going."

Annie did not budge. "We have to go back."

She is wacko! "Go back," complained Bradley, as a sickly, black-haired woman awkwardly hobbled past them. "I'm not going back. You won't even tell me what's yelling."

A large man with bushy, sandy-brown hair and glasses appeared from their left. "Hurry while you can," he said in a burly voice.

People wear glasses when they're dead, wondered Bradley. He held that question, addressing the pressing matter of a screaming monster.

"Well?" Bradley asked, his white ghost-eyes fixed on Annie.

"It's a Shriek," she replied. "They are dead, crazy people, and they don't look human anymore." As if hearing its name, the Shriek responded with a terrible wail. "And when you are close to them, they are so loud you can't even move. We have to go back."

Bradley was stunned. "No way! You know what's crazy? You! You are wacko. W-A-K-O-H. First, you tell me to run from the stupid thing. Then you say we have to go back, but if we do that, we can't even move?"

Annie lurched forward, matching the boy's outrage. "Listen to me, pee-wee. I think your sister and Benny are in danger."

Pee-wee? I'm not that small, thought Bradley. "How? You closed the mirror or the blue window or the door or whatever it is."

Annie moved closer and Bradley floated backward. "There are really bad things here. That Shriek is one of them. But the worst are Lost Souls. And they can open the doorway into your house. I think the Shriek stopped moving because he's guarding the door for them. We have to go back."

Another shriek from the Shriek shook the Nothing.

"Lost Souls," Bradley repeated quietly. "Do I want to know?"

Annie shook her head. "No. Now, let's go."

She turned and retraced their path. Bradley glided behind her, grasping his Hero Warrior sword at his side. Points of white light approached, growing larger and changing into people. They were men and women, dressed in the same flawless, white clothes. Some were old, and some were young, like Annie, but there were no children. As they passed, urgent warnings flew from their mouths.

"Turn around!"

"Run!"

"Follow us!"

Finally, no one passed. Only the dreadful sounds of the Shriek remained ahead, growing louder as Annie and Bradley returned.

In the distance, Bradley spotted a faint, bluish glow. *Sean's mirror,* he thought. As the doorway appeared in the distance, the still unseen creature let loose with a deafening scream. Annie flinched, wrapping her hands over her ears. Although the Shriek's cries were annoying and terribly loud, Bradley felt no pain. *Maybe it's because I'm a ghost,* he guessed.

"I'm not afraid," he whispered, floating behind Annie.

An enormous yell buckled her knees and she stumbled forward. “I’m not afraid,” repeated Bradley.

As they approached, he saw the pale-blue outline was gone, replaced by a brightly-lit, deep-blue rectangle. The mirror was open and Bradley momentarily pictured himself diving inside, until the monstrous figure guarding the entrance stepped in front.

The Shriek roared, sending a shock wave through them and across the Nothing. Annie's legs collapsed and she fell, curling up in pain on the formless ground. Impervious to the noise, Bradley stared at the monster. It looked much worse than the "dead, crazy person" Annie described. The Shriek's head appeared misshapen with bulging, red eyes partially covered by strands of fine, black hair. Its neck and body twisted in opposite directions, frenetically scanning the surrounding area. The Shriek's hands were clasped, its fingers wriggling like small snakes, nervously grasping at each other.

Thin, blood-red lips framed the Shriek's hideous mouth. The monster's coiled, pink tongue repeatedly lashed its crooked teeth. His mouth opened wide and directed a brutal howl at Bradley. Fearful, the boy considered shrinking away.

But I'm a ghost, he thought. *Which means you can't kill me.*

The Shriek cried out, again. Bradley remained firm. Thinking of Alyssa and Annie, Bradley summoned a mixture of courage and anger. Opening his white mouth, he imagined and expelled a long, booming shout, surprising himself with its ferocity.

The scream certainly startled the Shriek. Eyes wide and silenced, the ugly creature took a wary step backward.

"I am the *Hero Warrior*," screamed Bradley, raising his sword. "And I have you now!"

With a thunderous battle cry, he charged forward. The frightened Shriek bobbed, turned and ran. Bradley flew swiftly forward in pursuit, hollering as he chased the twisted figure. Unable to keep pace, he slowed and watched the Shriek scamper away into the depths of the Nothing.

Beaming, Bradley reveled in his triumph and enjoyed the quiet. Alone now, he realized how soundless it was in the Nothing. No airplanes. No cars. No children playing. No birds singing. Not even his breath to break the silence. *This is death*, he thought.

Bradley shook the morbid idea from his head and followed the blue glow back to Annie. She stood by the brilliantly-lit, rectangular portal, partially recovered from her confrontation and fall. Annie moved her hand across the doorway to the Dempsey home. The blue light faded into an outline, signaling the mirror's closure.

"Victory is ours," trumpeted Bradley. Much to his disappointment, Annie ignored him, finishing her task. "What happened?" he asked.

"The Lost Souls opened the mirror and went through," she replied. "That Shriek was guarding the entryway. I just closed it."

"You closed it?" yelled Bradley. "With Lost Souls in our house! Are you totally nuts?"

Annie shut her eyes, exhausted from the skirmish with the Shriek. "Lost Souls have no next life," she explained. "The Nothing is their only home. Without the mirror open, Lost Souls cannot exist in your world."

Annie's words failed to soothe Bradley. The Lost Souls already could have harmed his sister and Benny while the Shriek was guarding the mirror's entrance.

"They are nothing now," she continued.

"She says we're nothing," announced an unseen, raspy, irritated voice behind Annie. "That isn't very nice."

Chapter 5
The Lost Souls

Rascal, Mrs. Watson's pudgy, grey tabby, arched his back and hissed. Alone in the old woman's bedroom, Rascal recently replaced Dusty, a jet-black short-hair, as the watch-cat for any unusual activities in the Dempsey house. Minnie, the calico, remained within an earshot down the hall. Hearing Rascal, she leapt to the windowsill, joining her feline companion. After a quick peek, Minnie's back curved up and she spit fiercely at the glass.

Motionless in her bed, clasping the Essence to her pounding heart, Alyssa recalled her conversation earlier in the day and wondered whether Mrs. Watson's cats were staring at the shadowy figures in Sean's bedroom. That thought dissolved as the Lost Souls emerged from the mirror.

Alyssa peered into the darkness, struggling to see them. Rather than the misty forms of Annie and Benny, the Lost Souls appeared solid, looking more like people than ghosts. There were three, and they moved cautiously into the hallway. Alyssa prayed silently, suppressing the urge to cry out to Benny for help. One of the Lost Souls took a half-step toward her room, sniffing the stale air in front of him. Then he paused as the sound of Benny's laughter rose unexpectedly from downstairs. *More cartoons*, thought Alyssa.

A shadow in her doorway, the Lost Soul turned back and curled his finger toward the others. "This way," he whispered. "And keep your mouths closed."

All three slithered out of Alyssa's sight, sliding down the hall, following the television's faint sounds emanating from below. Remembering what Benny told her, the Lost Souls' departure increased Alyssa's panic.

They were people just like you and me, but they have no next life and they are really mean. And if they touch you, then you will never have a next life either.

Caught between her fear of moving and her concern for Benny, Alyssa remained frozen in bed, her shallow breaths punctuating indecision. Her head darted about, finally settling on a large, glass snow globe twinkling faintly on her dresser.

When she was eight, her father returned from a business trip to Denver with the snow globe, gently shaking the sphere and handing her the gift. Little Alyssa peered inside, finding white, plastic snowflakes swirling atop Bear Lake and the Rocky Mountains.

"Rosebud," he said, as she watched the liquid blizzard.

Frowning, eight-year-old Alyssa replied, "I don't see any roses." John Dempsey responded by patting his young daughter's head.

Ugly sounds of confrontation from the family room filtered through the floorboards beneath her bed, breaking the unnatural silence in Alyssa's room. *I have to do something*, she thought.

As a marginal measure of safekeeping, Alyssa tucked the Essence under her pillow and slid out of bed. Touching her feet to the floor, she quietly made her way across the bedroom. She stopped and collected the snow globe, the only weapon available. *At least it's heavy*, she thought. *Better than Bradley's plastic sword.* Raising the glass defensively, long dormant snowflakes began spinning in the dark.

"Rosebud," Alyssa whispered, hesitating. And then, thinking of her brothers and their own likely perils, she slipped into the hallway.

Creeping forward, the voices downstairs became more distinct. She heard a Lost Soul maliciously utter, ". . . or else, Benny." Reaching the top of the staircase, Alyssa dipped her head and listened intently.

"Maybe we should just touch him and get it over with," said another.

"Look, all Patrick wants is the Essence," spat the first. "She's the one that took it. Let her suffer."

He must be talking about Annie, thought Alyssa. Benny said Annie stole the glass wand, but now the Essence lay beneath her pillow. *Maybe I could trade it for my brothers*, wondered Alyssa. Embracing the possibility, she took a first, guarded step down the stairs.

"Talk, Benny," said the second. "And put your tongue back in your mouth. We don't have time for this crap."

Slowly descending the steps, Alyssa vacillated. Benny was in trouble, and she knew he would protect the Essence, even if it meant the Lost Souls touching him. But her brothers were trapped. And who cared about Annie? *I don't care about her*, she thought. Sean and Bradley were the priorities. *I have to get them home.*

In that uncertain mental swirl, Alyssa tried taking another distracted step down. Losing her balance, she tilted and fell to her left. Her body slammed against the stairway wall, the noise echoing for a moment and then replaced by a dreadful stillness, quickly enveloping the entire house. With her body angled against the wall, she remained motionless, fighting the sudden urge to cry out for her mother.

Alyssa's eyes latched onto the yellow-pine foyer floor, reflecting the light coming from the kitchen. Waiting for a reaction to her fall, her ears sharpened, singularly filled by the heartbeat ticking of the Dempsey's grandfather clock standing guard in their living room. Alyssa added more promises to those made the previous night. *I'll go to church every Sunday. I won't hide candy in my closet. I'll help Mom do the laundry. Anything, anything, anything*, she thought. *Please, save me.*

The foyer floor changed. Strands of light broke and shifted, and an eerie shadow stretched across the wood tiles. A Lost Soul. *Please, save me.* A Lost Soul was moving toward her.

"Alyssa, run!" shouted Benny.

Alyssa turned and sprinted upwards, reaching the top of the stairs and scurrying down the hall, banging into the walls as she flew. *Through the mirror*, she thought desperately. It was the only escape.

Bounding into Sean's room, she rushed to the dresser, the mirror's liquid surface beckoning her inside. But with her leg half-raised, a terrible thought occurred. *The wand! The Essence!* It was in her room, under the pillow.

Despite her certainty that she had no time to recover it, Alyssa spun around. She was right. Before Alyssa took a step, a Lost Soul appeared in the doorway, barring her exit. He was slightly taller than her with wavy, black hair and deep-set, serious eyes. In the darkness, his formless clothes exuded a murky, purplish radiance. As the Lost Soul crept into Sean's room, the mirror's glow exposed his entire body, dressed in fiery red, with no seams or breaks evident. The soft, blue light of Sean's digital clock revealed a youthful face, layered with deep wrinkles, as if the Lost Soul had aged prematurely.

Alyssa recoiled as another Lost Soul appeared, similarly clothed, with short, spiky hair, the same thick creases across his face, and a terrible, evil grin.

"We're not going to hurt you," said the first.

Alyssa lifted the snow globe in a feeble act of self-defense, which her pursuers ignored. The second Lost Soul stared quizzically at the glass sphere.

"Alyssa, don't give it to them," cried Benny, arriving at the bedroom door. Behind him, a third Lost Soul stood hidden, except for the violet glow of his clothes sifting through the Benny's cloudy body.

"Keep your mouth shut," shouted the first. Benny winced, covering his face.

"Desmond," said the second, wagging a finger at the snow globe. "That's not it."

Desmond's black eyes narrowed, spotting plastic snowflakes whirling about inside the glass. "Where's the Essence?" he barked at Alyssa. "Where is the –"

"Look," yelled the third, sneaking around Benny. He pointed at the wall over Alyssa's head. She turned, seeing only the Spiderman sign with the words "Sean's Room" printed inside the web. Alyssa spun her head back. All three Lost Souls gaped at the sign.

"Who's Sean?" demanded Desmond.

Alyssa locked eyes with Benny. *What's going on*, she mouthed. He shook his head at her.

"Is Sean your brother?"

Alyssa stood mutely, frightened that anything she said might jeopardize her brothers, lost somewhere on the other side of the mirror. Benny waved a chalky, white hand, urging silence.

"Enough of this!" growled Desmond. Pointing an index finger, he reached out to Benny. Panicked, the ghost floated backward. The third Lost Soul slid behind him, barring his escape.

"One touch from me and you can kiss your fat friend goodbye," threatened Desmond. "You have three seconds to start talking. Begin by telling me where I can find the Essence and why I am standing in Sean's room!"

Alyssa had no options. *If don't say something, Benny won't have a next life.*

"One."

If I answer, they might hurt Sean and Bradley.

"Two."

Desmond's wrinkled fingertip cut through the darkness, approaching Benny.

"Stop," screamed Alyssa, hurling the snow globe at Desmond. At the same moment, the deflating hiss of a huge, unseen rubber ball filled the bedroom. All three Lost Souls cried out as their bodies began evaporating.

Her father's glass gift hurtled toward Desmond, traveling through his fading, smoky figure. Alyssa saw the soaring snow globe's reflection, approaching the mirror. *It's solid*, she thought, as the object and image collided.

In Mrs. Watson's bedroom, Rascal and Minnie leapt from the windowsill, the sound of the mirror shattering permanently and chasing the curious cats from their post. Joined by Dusty, the trio scampered to the basement, remaining rooted in their deep hiding places until the old woman coaxed them out, many hours later, with a large bowl of tuna.

In Sean's room, three Lost Souls released a final howl, disappearing beneath a shower of glass spraying on the floor. Alyssa and Benny were suddenly alone, two points of a large triangle with the third being the mirror's splintered remains. Their uncertain eyes met and Alyssa felt the sting of tears. *I know what he's going to say.*

Benny's mouth unhinged and his familiar words filled the space between them.

"This is not a good thing."

Chapter 6
Patrick

"They are nothing now," said Annie.

"She says we're nothing. That isn't very nice."

Annie and Bradley turned, facing a Lost Soul. Others, all wearing red, emerged from the blackness and surrounded them. But the looming confrontation abruptly ended. Behind Annie, the portal to Sean's bedroom emitted a blinding burst of blue light, followed by a shock wave, knocking everyone to their knees, with the exception of Bradley who spun in circles.

"Annie!" he shouted, rapidly blinking his blinded eyes. Bright blue spots obliterated the dark Nothing. Faring no better, the temporarily sightless Lost Souls stumbled about. Shielded from the light burst, Annie jumped to her feet.

"Just do what they say," she whispered into Bradley's ear.

"What?" He whipped his head around, and stuck out his hands, searching for her. "Annie? Annie?"

Surrounding Bradley, the Lost Souls slowly recovered. "What happened?" yelled one.

Another shouted, "Wallace, the gate's gone!"

The Lost Soul who first spoke behind Annie and Bradley rose and shook his head. "I can see that," he sneered.

Bradley's vision finally cleared, revealing Wallace's face.

The man had sinister, sooty eyes, which held no patience. He seemed about the same age as Bradley's father, but his jaw and cheeks were painted with deep, disfiguring wrinkles.

"The girl's gone, too," said a female voice. Bradley scanned the group. There were eight Lost Souls, three of whom were women. They were dressed in the same seamless clothes as Annie, but theirs were colored bright red. Their scarred, grey faces looked as unhappy as Wallace.

"I can see that. You stay here, Kir. The rest of you, go look for her!" Wallace barked.

No one hesitated. Except for Kir, the Lost Souls scurried off in separate directions.

Bradley watched them disappear into the blackness. The Nothing swallowed the Lost Souls' red glow much faster than Annie and those dressed in white. Swiveling in the darkness, Bradley examined Wallace and Kir. Blood-red shone from their clothes, but their blemished skin was shadowy and dull, giving off no light at all. Bradley raised his white ghost-hand. It shimmered, illuminating the area around him.

Only the Lost Souls' clothes glow, thought Bradley. *Their bodies have no light.*

"Patrick's going to have us for this," Kir said when the others were gone.

Wallace eyed Bradley. "Well? Where did she go?"

Looking down, Bradley realized he was still holding his sword. The triumph over the Shriek surged fresh in his mind. He raised the sword, cried courageously, and charged.

"I am the *Hero Warrior*!"

The ghost-boy soared, quickly covering the short distance and plunging a pale, shimmering sword into Wallace's chest. The smoky toy popped out of the Lost Soul's back without any discernible effects. Bradley halted, flashing Wallace an embarrassed grin.

"I really don't have time for this," said Wallace, annoyed. He placed a withered, creased hand into the boy, erasing Bradley's smile. A thousand invisible needles burst from the Lost Soul's fingers, searing the teenager. Bradley's misty body shuddered on an endless scream.

I'm dying!

The Nothing disappeared.

* * *

Bradley's white eyelids fluttered open. Oddly angled and slowly twisting in a circle, he floated limply near Wallace and Kir.

"Ow," he said quietly, suffering from the terrible pain of Wallace's attack.

Kir hooted an insensitive laugh. Unamused, Wallace shot her a disapproving look. Kir's wicked smile dissolved. Wallace approached Bradley, who shifted himself upright. *Not again*, he thought, bracing for more.

"Where did she go?" Wallace demanded.

"I don't know," responded Bradley. "After the blue thing exploded, she said 'do what they say' and that was it." Wallace looked unconvinced. "I'm telling the truth. I'll tell you whatever you want to know, okay? Just don't do that needle thing to me again."

"They're coming back," interrupted Kir, pointing at scattered red lights moving toward them. They waited silently as the other Lost Souls arrived, each one reporting the same thing. Annie had vanished.

"What a wonderful friend who leaves you like that," said Wallace sarcastically, before addressing his companions. "Patrick's waiting. Let's go."

Bradley did not bother to ask where. As the group traveled through the Nothing, he scouted around, wondering if escape was possible. *I could just fly off*, he thought. *I'm fast.* But the painful memory of those horrible, burning needles dissuaded him from acting recklessly.

"That's a scary sword," joked one of the Lost Souls. A few of the others laughed. Bradley gritted his transparent teeth.

"He tried to attack Wallace with it," added Kir. "He lifted the sword and said he was a warrior and then Wallace pinned him." Everyone snickered, except Wallace and Bradley.

"Maybe he's not a boy," said another woman, her foul, black hair dangling across scarred, grey cheeks. "Maybe he's just a baby soldier. Are you? Are you a baby soldier?"

"Shut up," yelled Bradley, seething. The Lost Souls chanted "oo" in unison.

"I agree with the kid. Shut up!" snapped Wallace, wiping away the Lost Souls' menacing, wrinkled smiles. "I have enough to think about right now without you morons cackling away. Now, keep quiet."

The group plodded on. Bradley anxiously watched Wallace as they proceeded silently.

If this guy is worried, he thought, *then this Patrick is probably going to be mad at me. And I didn't even do anything. It was Annie who gave Sean the wand. And it was Sean's fault for being stupid enough to go into the mirror. And it's Alyssa's fault for letting me get stuck here.*

Ahead, Bradley saw what looked like short, bright-red, neon lines. As they approached, the lines merged into crimson triangles, which formed a huge, patterned dome. Thirty or forty more Lost Souls moved outside the brightly-lit structure, some heading off into the Nothing, and others speaking with a tall man standing nearby. *Patrick*, thought Bradley.

"This way," ordered Wallace.

He led the teenager to Patrick, whom Bradley immediately recognized as the man in white with Annie when he passed through the mirror. The boy's eyes narrowed. *There's something different about him.*

Like the Lost Souls, Patrick was dressed in flawless red. But the resemblance ended there. Patrick's intense, young face was smooth, and his entire body was shrouded with a flaming glow. A halo of scarlet outlined his thick, slicked-back, deep-brown hair.

Bradley felt the same familiarity he experienced with the man in white. *I know him*, he thought. *But this guy's different. He's bad news.*

A darker, dimmer Wallace slid behind his leader, and they both examined Bradley. Wallace's eyes flicked about, while Patrick sharply studied the boy. Bradley waited patiently, concluding that Patrick was no Lost Soul.

"Who is the kid?" he asked finally. Identical only in tone, Patrick's voice commanded strict authority, lacking the compassion of the man in white.

"He must have crossed over, Patrick," answered Wallace. He recounted the explosion, Annie's disappearance, and his attack on Bradley. His voice faltered at times, and the other Lost Souls guarding the boy dropped their heads as Wallace spoke. *They're all afraid of Patrick*, thought Bradley.

"Did you ask him any questions?" grumbled Patrick, when Wallace finished. No one responded.

"So instead of delivering the thief and the mailman, you bring me news of a burst gate and some kid stupid enough to climb through before it blew, without even finding out who he is and where he came from!"

"What's your name?" Patrick asked.

"Bradley," he whispered.

"You know what you're going to do for me now, Brad? You're going to nod your head every time I say something that's right. Is that understood?"

Bradley hated being called Brad, particularly the way Patrick spat out his name. He sounded like Alyssa teasing him. Wisely, Bradley remained silent and merely nodded.

"Do you remember the pain you felt when he pinned you?" asked Patrick, pointing at Wallace. "If you lie to me, I'm going to pin you myself. And when I pin someone, he never opens his eyes again."

Patrick's warning loomed ominously and Bradley had no interest in testing the man's patience. "I won't lie," said Bradley quietly.

"Good," replied Patrick. "Now, I have a strange feeling that two ghosts came through a mirror in your house. Yes?"

Bradley nodded. Yes.

"A thin woman and a fat man?"

Once more, Bradley nodded.

"Incredible," said Patrick, glaring at Wallace and the other Lost Souls. "You ask simple questions and you get simple answers. Was that difficult?"

"No," replied Wallace submissively.

Patrick returned to Bradley. "And they left behind a red light which you thought was some kind of magic toy?"

"It was glass with red stuff inside," said Bradley. "Like a wand."

"A glass wand," said Patrick, intrigued. "Hmm. Very interesting. I just learned something else."

"Yes, sir," added Bradley, hoping formality might help.

"Manners. I appreciate that," Patrick continued in a patronizing tone. "But at some point you climbed through the mirror?"

Bradley nodded. Honesty was working, and "yes" or "no" questions made this easy. He considered telling Patrick that they met when he came through, but Bradley was certain that Patrick and the man in white were two different people. *Either that or this guy's playing a really weird game.*

"Why did you come through?"

So much for "yes" or "no" questions. The truth's better than being pinned.

"To find my little brother. He climbed through first," replied Bradley.

Patrick gazed at the Lost Souls. "Any other kids?"

They all shook their heads.

"Just him. And Annie," added Wallace.

"Yes." Patrick's menacing, black eyes narrowed, and his mouth filled with venom. "Annie."

I wonder if he'd pin me if I asked to go home, thought Bradley.

"What's your brother's name?"

"Sean."

Patrick's face tightened, and Kir gasped. Sean's name stilled the entire red-cloaked group. Bradley's head whirled from Patrick to the others, desperate for an answer.

Oh, no! Did I say the wrong thing?

"What?" whispered Patrick, breaking the silence.

"Sean," repeated Bradley. *Why do they care about his name? Something pretty bad is going to happen to me.* "I don't really like him," he added meekly.

A solemn Patrick crept closer. His bullying face dipped down, hovering barely an inch over Bradley's milky-white, quivering nose. The dead man's breathless words were slow and deliberate.

"Let's start from the beginning."

* * *

Alyssa slept in Sean's bed, while the Essence, held to her chest, rose and fell with her rhythmic breathing. Beside her, Benny floated, standing guard over the teenager and the shattered glass covering the carpet. Alyssa had neither the heart nor the energy to clean up the mess. She cried and questioned and even cursed at Benny, searching for answers to the Lost Souls' reaction when they discovered they were in Sean's room.

"I don't know," he repeated as she interrogated him.

Alyssa became less convinced with each denial that Benny was clueless. *And for good reason*, thought Benny, as he watched Alyssa sleeping. *All I have told you since this morning are half-truths and lies.*

There were two things Benny did not know. What was the plan now that the mirror was gone? And what were Annie, Sean, and Bradley doing? Benny wished he could sleep.

While he fretted, downstairs in the Dempsey house, tiny flecks of white, fibrous mold sprouted upon the topmost pancakes stacked on the kitchen table. *Charlotte's Web* remained on the couch, lying where Alyssa dropped it after her earlier confrontation with Benny.

And on the family room wall, the glass inside the oval mirror faded, replaced by a star-filled, liquid shimmer.

The Essence
Book III
Sunday and the Brothers
Vel Grande
Illustrations by Krystle Carkeek

"I have no idea where this will lead us,
but I have a definite feeling it will be a place
both wonderful and strange."

Agent Dale Cooper, *Twin Peaks*

Chapter 1
Sean

"So, do you guys ever smile?"

Determining time in the perpetual night surrounding him was impossible. Bradley guessed that an hour had passed since the search for Annie began. But he really had no idea. Worse yet, Bradley was terribly bored. Monotony always made time slow to a crawl, particularly in the unending emptiness of the Nothing. And there were only so many times he could count the neon-red triangles creating the brightly lit dome in which he was guarded.

Before departing with all the others in large, red-clad bands, Patrick handed Bradley off to two Lost Souls. The thirteen-year-old boy initially respected his captors by remaining silent, until boredom finally broke his patience.

"What?" sneered one of them.

Bradley was old enough to understand that answers like "what?" to the questions of children did not mean "please repeat your question." Rather, "what?" usually meant, "why are you talking to me?" or simply "be quiet." Unfortunately, Bradley was still young enough to disregard caution.

"Do you guys ever smile? Oh, and I counted. Eighty-four triangles," announced Bradley proudly, pointing at the dome. "Can you guys count?"

He tried apologizing as the Lost Soul's wrinkled hand

plunged into him, but Bradley's voice drowned in searing pain. From every direction, thin, unseen spikes pierced his ghost body. The hot stinging swept through Bradley's convulsing torso, while he begged wordlessly for the pain to end.

Finally, the Lost Soul withdrew, concluding the nightmare. Still conscious and drifting limply in the darkness, Bradley wondered why he was awake.

When Wallace pinned me, he knocked me out, he thought. *If Wallace is stronger, I'm never getting Patrick mad.*

As he recovered, Bradley remembered his answers to Patrick's questions. He told Patrick about the glass wand, the bicycle, and the purple apple. And about Annie, Benny, and the mirror. But mostly, Bradley answered questions about Sean until he was certain that either his brother was special, or Patrick was a little strange. *Probably both,* Bradley thought.

"Just do what they say," Annie instructed, before abandoning him to the Lost Souls. Bradley followed her advice, but he avoided mentioning the man in white. The man he saw when he first came through the mirror. The man who looked like Patrick.

"Any more questions?" asked the Lost Soul that pinned him. Bradley shook his head and returned to his thoughts, silently counting triangles again.

What's so special about Sean? he wondered. *I'm the one suffering!*

Bradley resolved to punish Sean once they got home. But how? Cleaning up the pancakes was a good place to start.

I'm not cleaning them up, he thought. *I could be playing* Hero Warrior *right now. Instead I'm stuck, stuck, stuck in this stupid place!*

"I hate you, Sean," Bradley muttered quietly.

"Join the crowd," said the other Lost Soul. His youthful face was layered with scars, but his voice lacked malice.

He's sort of sad, thought Bradley.

"Put a lid on it, Cade!" his companion shouted. "Unless you want Patrick on you for not doing what he said."

"You're right, Simon," replied Cade sourly. "We don't want to get Patrick mad. Who'd want to lose this place? It's paradise."

The two Lost Souls eyed each other. Certain of an impending fight, Bradley studied his surroundings for an escape route. But neither Lost Soul moved. Slowly they relaxed, returning to their guard duties.

They hate Sean, too, realized Bradley. This was a new development. *What did Sean do? He just got here. Maybe they're reading my mind?* Bradley quickly packed his brain with spiteful thoughts of his four-year-old brother.

An explosion in the distance rippled through the Nothing, echoing loudly and reminding Bradley of a train in a tunnel. As the clattering wave passed, the triangles in the dome faded from red to white.

"Can I go now?" asked Bradley, while counting anew, in case both the number and the color of triangles changed.

Cade turned on him. "What did you do?" he demanded fiercely.

"Really?" replied Bradley. "What did I do? I came through the stupid mirror or the gate or whatever it is. That's all I did, okay? I don't live here. I'm trying to find my brother, Sean. Remember him?"

"Look," said Simon, pointing his finger into the blackness. Cade and Bradley turned. In the dark, shadowy distance, a bright point of white light appeared, growing larger and moving toward them. "Do you think it's her?"

Cade scratched his head. "I don't know."

Simon shifted back and forth. "Maybe it's best not to find out," he said.

"We can take her."

Bradley laughed and the two Lost Souls turned, seeking an explanation. "I barely know her, but if that's Annie, I sure wouldn't want to fight her."

Cade and Simon held their ground, closed ranks on Bradley, and waited. The young teenage boy silently wished for Annie, but not as his savior.

I am going to totally yell at you for leaving me with these jerks.

The trio watched the light gradually stretch into a figure, finally transitioning into Patrick. He left like the other Lost

Souls, dressed in scarlet, but now Patrick returned clothed in seamless white. The dome's glow flickered as he crossed its threshold and approached them.

"Both of you," he barked at Cade and Simon. "Go check on the others. They're in the half-circle."

Bradley examined Patrick's face. The anger remained, but the intensity was gone, along with his vivid, blood-red halo. His black eyes appeared a shade lighter, and their cold, threatening gaze seemed forced.

That's not Patrick, Bradley realized. *It's the other man.*

"What happened?" asked Cade.

Bradley wondered if Cade was questioning the explosion or the change in color.

"We caught her. I'll explain the rest later." The Lost Souls hesitated. Bradley sensed their uncertainty. Cade and Simon knew something was amiss, but neither wanted to risk challenging the man.

"What about him?" asked Simon, pointing at Bradley.

"I think I can handle him. Now go!"

The Lost Souls jumped with fear and ran off. Bradley watched them dissolve into the Nothing, finally disappearing from sight. He remained cautious, grasping at the white, misty sword handle by his side, still uncertain if this was Patrick.

"Are you all right?" the man asked.

"I knew it was you," said Bradley, his body flooding with warm relief.

"The two of them suspected me as well," replied the man. "Luckily, my appearance carries a nasty reputation."

"Who are you? Where's my brother? Why did you leave? Why did Annie leave me? I'm really mad about that," huffed Bradley. "They hurt me!"

"I'm sorry," said the man. "Our plan changed a little

when you came through. And it changed a lot after the gate was destroyed. I promise not to leave you again. But we need to go. Annie's waiting for us and right now we're in danger."

Without waiting for a response, the man turned and sprinted out of the dome. Bradley floated behind, rushing to catch up. As he reached the man, the light around them shifted. Looking back, Bradley saw the reason. Once again, the Dome's color burned red.

"It changed back," said Bradley.

"I know."

"What was that noise?" asked Bradley, floating alongside of the man as he ran.

"A distraction."

Bradley stopped. The man jogged another few paces before turning around and stopping, too.

"What are you doing?" he asked Bradley.

"So, I think you're good, but I don't really know you. Or Annie." Bradley collected his thoughts. He hated being confused. "I mean, who's Patrick? And why do you look like him?"

The man came closer, offering a smile. "I understand. I promise you'll get answers to all of your questions."

"The noise?" demanded Bradley, crossing his ghost arms.

"I made it. The Nothing looks empty to you, but those who are dead see it differently. Above us it is filled with streams of energy. The streams are colored bands and they are very strong. If they break, there is an explosion while the energy moves to another stream."

"I don't understand," said Bradley.

"I broke a white stream and funneled it into a red one. That's why you heard that sound, and that's why the Arena, the big dome you were inside of, turned white."

Bradley nodded his head, pretending the story made sense. "Why can't I see the streams?"

"Because you are alive," explained the man. "You see death the way it should be seen. Cold and black. But the people here are all dead. And they see colored paths above the darkness that should return them to a new life."

"Well, you're dead. Can you see the colors?" asked Bradley, trying his best to comprehend.

The man shifted uncomfortably. "Sort of."

"You can sort of see the colors?" asked Bradley.

"No. I am sort of . . . dead," replied the man.

"What?" shouted Bradley. "You are sort of dead? What does that mean? Are you sort of alive? Are you sort of good and sort of bad?"

"Look," the man said cautiously. "We really need to keep moving. The longer I stand here answering your questions, the harder it will become for me to get you home."

Only me, thought Bradley. "What about Sean?"

"And Sean," the man added indifferently.

Whoa! And Sean? Something is totally wrong. This guy left me! Annie left me! And now he doesn't even care about Sean?

"I'm not going anywhere until I know who you are," Bradley demanded.

The man lowered his head. "Bradley, we need to go."

"I'm not going anywhere," repeated the boy, forcefully, "unless it's to find my brother! Where is he?"

"Bradley, we need to go."

"Who are you?" Bradley crossed his arms and waited for an answer.

"I'm Patrick's brother. His twin brother," said the man, his black eyes still lowered, fixed on the cold, formless ground.

He paused, released a breathless sigh, and raised his head.

"And I'm your brother, Bradley. I'm Sean."

Chapter 2
Will

Alyssa Dempsey blazed around the walnut kitchen table, scooping up moldy pancakes and dumping them into large, yellow, plastic garbage bags. She tossed in thirty or forty at a time, but when she turned back to the table, the stacks were inexplicably larger than before. Worse, her head was pounding, a product of the racket emanating from the family room.

"I am the *Hero Warrior*!" blared the television repeatedly.

I hate that game, thought Alyssa.

She spun around, intending to yell at Bradley and have him lower the sound, but he was not there. Bradley. Sean. They were still gone. How could she be so stupid? Alyssa spent the last hour unsuccessfully cleaning up the kitchen table and forgot to look for her brothers.

And where is Benny?

In the foyer, the front door opened with a rattling crash that shook the house. Alyssa cautiously peered down the hallway.

Oh no, she thought, feeling her heart deflate.

Standing in the doorway were her mother and father. John Dempsey's coal-black eyes fixed on his daughter, and his mouth twisted with a disapproving scowl. Next to him, Leslie Dempsey wore the same rigid, infuriated expression she bore when she caught a four-year-old Alyssa drawing magic-marker happy faces on the dining room wall, many years ago.

Alyssa's mother held up an accusing fist. Beads of dark-red blood formed at her thumb, trickling down her wrist, and dripping to the floor. Leslie opened her wounded hand. A piece of a shattered reflective glass lay in embedded in her palm.

"Why did you break Sean's mirror?" screeched her mother. "Where are your brothers?"

"I don't know," whimpered Alyssa. Ashamed, she cast her eyes to the floor. Piled around her feet were more rotting pancakes. Stacks of them wound around her legs, latching on to her calves and thighs like the ivy on the brick chimney outside their home.

"Where is the Essence?" her father demanded, frightening Alyssa.

How did they know about the Essence?

The Lost Soul, Desmond, appeared, ascending from behind her parents and triumphantly holding the glass wand above his head. His wrinkled faced beamed, and his black eyes ignited into yellow-red flames dancing maliciously in the darkness.

How could I have lost the Essence? Did I put it down?

Desmond raised the Essence higher, preparing to strike her mother and father.

"No!" cried Alyssa.

The Lost Soul opened his mouth as if to laugh, but the only sound that emerged was the persistent chirping tone of Alyssa's cell phone, alerting her that she had received a new text message. Opening her eyes, the teenager bolted up in her brother Sean's bed. Beads of sweat dotted her forehead. She wiped them away as the dream faded and the living nightmare returned.

Alyssa checked her other hand to make sure she still held the Essence, but there was no real need. She could feel the smooth, cold glass pressing against her palm. The wand never seemed warm, no matter how long Alyssa squeezed it.

Floating nearby with a concerned, puffy-white face was Benny. And through his hazy body, she could see the door to her room, out of which the electronic sounds of her cell phone pulsed.

"It's been doing that for a while," remarked Benny.

"What time is it?" Alyssa asked.

"Almost eleven."

Exhausted, Alyssa moaned and dropped her head. Her parents returned home today. The end was near, bringing with it a terrible conclusion to the weekend.

"What are we going to do?" she asked desperately.

Benny tried to respond, but through a contorted ghost face all he could utter was "um," and "well," until he finally gave up.

"I'll be downstairs," he said unhappily and floated out of Sean's room.

Alyssa's mouth flapped open as she toyed with the idea of yelling at Benny. But there was no point. Every plan Alyssa crafted to bring first Sean and then Bradley back home lay in ruins like the shattered, sparkling pieces of mirror on the carpet. With the Essence in her hand, Alyssa slid out of bed and carefully made her way through a sea of broken glass to retrieve her cell phone from her own room.

Seventeen text messages!

The list began with Will's declarations of love, followed by a couple asking, "IS EVERYTHING OKAY?" There were three messages from friends, which Alyssa scrolled through without opening. And then she reached the last two. One was from her mom.

"See you at 3. That gives you time to clean up the house."

The other was sent by Will.

"I'M HOME. I'LL STOP BY AROUND 11."

Eleven!

A car door closed outside. Rushing to her window, Alyssa saw Will's rust-spotted, white Ford parked in their driveway. She caught a glimpse of his head disappearing beneath the porch awning.

"Oh, no," whined Alyssa as the doorbell rang.

She raced down the hall, stopping in the bathroom to

survey the effects of the weekend in the mirror. The last time Alyssa saw herself was Friday, when she ran to meet Will before he left to visit his grandparents. Surveying the effects of the last two days was not pleasant. Alyssa still wore the same grey sweats. Her stained white t-shirt was now lined with dark, dried, perspiration marks. Her blue eyes were submerged beneath a pool of bloodshot vessels. And a small, scabbed cut inched down the side of her neck, probably the result of Sean's mirror shattering.

"And I haven't taken a shower since Thursday," said Alyssa to her reflection. She considered sniffing her t-shirt, but unhappily concluded that doing so would depress her further.

Alyssa tugged at the long, unwashed tangles of her dark-brown hair, but there was no quick fix to the damage done.

What will Will think? she thought. *And what about Benny? There's no explaining him.*

The doorbell rang again and Alyssa vaulted down the steps, still trying to formulate a plan of action. She decided to dismiss Will and repair his bruised ego later. But excuses came to her like water in the desert. By the time she landed in the foyer, Alyssa held nothing other than the front door handle, which she mindlessly turned.

Will's uneasy smile faded at the sight of his girlfriend. "Oh my God! You look terrible."

"I love you too," Alyssa responded sarcastically, planting her hands on her hips. Momentarily, she kept a cool exterior, until her bottom lip quivered and she burst into tears, collapsing into Will's body. Stepping into the Dempsey home, Will wrapped his arms around Alyssa.

"I'm sorry," said Will, stroking her hair. "What happened?"

Will heard the muffled word "everything" through Alyssa's sobbing. As he tucked his head down toward her body, Will's nose wrinkled. She smelled like a pile of old, sweaty socks.

"I thought maybe some serial killer offed you and your brothers," said Will, consoling Alyssa with a joke. She faked a small laugh and pulled away, dabbing at her eyes as she straightened up.

"I'm sure I look worse now. And I probably stink, too."

"No you don't," lied Will. "What happened?"

Alyssa drew a deep breath and put her right hand on Will's arm. Finally, she had someone in whom she could confide the insanity of the weekend. Would he believe her? Alyssa did not care. A wave of calm washed across her as she prepared to bare her soul. And then, from the family room, Benny laughed.

Will's brow knotted and his eyes surveyed Alyssa's face.

"Actually," she said slowly. "This is not the best time. Can you come back a little –"

Will slid past Alyssa, moving swiftly down the foyer toward the kitchen. Stacks of cold, stale pancakes piled on the kitchen table greeted him, but Will paused with a raised eyebrow before turning toward the source of the laugh he heard. Alyssa anxiously pursued him, desperately shouting "Wait!"

Will surveyed the vacant family room, finding nothing other than the television broadcasting a nacho chips commercial. Maybe it was an actor's laugh. He leaned against the wood-paneled wall and made a quizzical face at Alyssa, who stood warily by the kitchen table, holding the glistening, bright-red Essence by her side.

What's the deal with the pancakes? Will thought. *And what's that glass thing in her hand?*

"Sorry," he said in an uncertain voice. "For a second I thought you had a new boyfriend."

"New boyfriend!" shouted Benny, emerging from the wall by Will with a huge, white smile. "I wish!"

With the wide-eyed look of a pursued animal, Will recoiled from the floating phantom. Benny reached out, offering to shake the young man's hand. Will responded with a wild punch at the ghost's extended white, puffy arm. When he swung through Benny without striking flesh, Will let out a high-pitched screech and dashed to the far side of the family room.

"Stop it," shouted Alyssa. "You're scaring him."

"I'm just playing," complained Benny.

"What's going on?" cried Will to Alyssa, clenching his fists in the corner. "What is that?"

"You're scaring him, Benny!"

"Benny?" repeated Will. "Who's Benny?"

"I am not scaring him." The ghost floated in front of Will, bobbing in the air with a silly grin. "You see," he said to Alyssa.

Benny's cloudy eyes sparkled.

"Boo!" he shouted.

Will leapt away, his back slamming against the wall next to the family room mirror, which cast no reflection of the collision. Alyssa prepared to reprimand the portly ghost, but her eyes shifted to the shimmering oval surface that replaced the mirror's glass. Benny's smile faded, and he drifted toward Alyssa, joining her and gazing uneasily at the new portal.

Will twisted his body to see the object of their fascination. Cool air rose from the glossy, black veneer. An electric chill filled his nose.

It's beautiful, he thought, mesmerized.

“It’s filled with stars,” Will whispered. “I can touch them.”

Alyssa and Benny watched as Will extended his hand. They both opened their mouths, but their mutual warning fell silently from their lips as Annie’s pale, white face burst through the twinkling, black surface. Will cried out and fell to the carpeted floor by his girlfriend’s feet. Annie ignored him. Instead, she found Alyssa holding what she wanted.

“The Essence! Give it to me,” Annie shouted, thrusting her arm toward the startled girl.

"What?" mouthed Alyssa, protectively gripping the glass wand.

"Your brothers are in danger. Give it to me now!"

Reluctantly, Alyssa held out the Essence. Annie's vaporous hand snatched it away. Without another word, she turned and disappeared noiselessly back through the mirror. It remained open and undisturbed. Small points of white light glimmered on its dark face.

"What's going on?" demanded Will, lying on the floor and trying to catch his breath.

Neither Alyssa nor Benny answered. Motionless, they stared at the mirror, quietly mourning the loss of the magical wand they endeavored to protect.

No brothers and now no Essence, thought Alyssa.

Her turbulent weekend was suddenly hollow and insignificant, reduced to an overweight ghost, a petrified boyfriend, and a house in ruins. Alyssa considered following Annie into the Nothing, but found no real purpose in the idea, other than escaping the impending wrath of her parents' return.

"Hello?" repeated Will frantically. "Can you please tell me what is going on?"

"Boo," said Benny flatly.

Fresh tears snaked down Alyssa's unwashed cheeks.

Chapter 3
A Time Past

After Annie's sudden departure, a perplexed and anxious Will comforted Alyssa, while he tried to make sense of the morning's events. Benjamin Evechikowski, the ghostly source of Will's nervous confusion, slowly floated in circles, lost in his own thoughts. Benny reflected on a time when he stood alone in the Nothing, wondering if he had reached the designated meeting place that Sean described.

Above Benny was one of two places in the Nothing where a red stream of energy twisted around a white stream, forming a tight braid. It reminded him of the way his wife's ponytail of soft, auburn hair meandered down her neck and back.

Benny missed his wife terribly. He no longer knew how much time had passed since he died. There was no sleeping in the Nothing. No eating. No breathing. Imagine speaking, he was told by others when he woke up after the accident. But when he spoke, a lifeless, woody taste coated his tongue.

Months before, his U.S. Mail truck had stalled on a small, rural county road at the edge of his delivery route. It would not start again and the radio was out. *Probably a dead battery*, he thought.

Benny believed it was good fortune when a bright-red Jeep pulled over in a soft cloud of dust. Patrick and Sean, twin brothers, introduced themselves, and after Benny told them what had happened, they offered him a ride back to the post office. Sean's wife Annie made room in the rear seat. She talked with Benny as they drove and he liked her instantly.

Then a loud horn sounded. Benny saw a large, metallic-brown truck to his right, heard a crash, and for a second, he felt the worst pain in his life. He blacked out and awoke in the Nothing next to Patrick, Sean, and Annie, all of them wearing the same seamless, white clothes.

Much of their early time together was spent understanding the Nothing. Its black surface and colorful, streaked, low-level atmosphere stretched infinitely in every direction. Patrick and Sean began tracking intersections of the colored streams above. Traveling for what seemed like days while following the distinct, vivid patterns, they realized the lines always returned them back to where they started. The Nothing was a huge sphere.

The four of them were far from alone. This new world was populated with hundreds, and possibly thousands, of dead people, with more arriving each hour. But the Nothing was still large enough to travel long distances without crossing paths with anyone else.

Those who were dead the longest spoke of two areas where people disappeared into descending colored streams, echoing with the sound of a human heart. Both places, which were set apart on opposite sides of the Nothing, contained braids of red and white energy flowing above. However, for unknown reasons, neither of the braids had lowered in a long time. Crowds of dead people waiting beneath them were disbanding, looking for other ways out of the unending darkness.

A few of the people they met explained that by using their thoughts, they could create gateways through mirrors in the world of the living. Annie became particularly adept at making the light blue doors, which marked the points of access. But no one found comfort crossing back over. All they created was terrible fear, even when they found the homes of their loved ones. Benny considered looking for his house to see his wife but decided against the plan. Ghosts were not welcome.

One calming aspect of the Nothing was that each inhabitant gave off a glow of soft, white light. And each glow was slightly distinct in its shape. Benny could see Sean and Annie in the distance and recognize who it was before each of them arrived. They wondered whether this was their souls. Or perhaps it was some individual reflection of the white beams streaming above them through the darkness.

There was one exception to the uniqueness of each person's light. The ones radiating from Sean and Patrick were identical.

"It must be a twin thing," guessed Annie.

"At least you married the one with more money," joked Sean.

"A lot of good that does me now," she replied.

As the unrelenting, sleepless time continued, the group of four divided and explored more of the Nothing. Benny preferred pairing up with Annie. She was smart and pretty, with long, dark hair sliding down her face, partially covering her right eye and cheek.

And she likes my jokes, he thought.

During one of their excursions, the streams of light overhead flashed brightly and all of them turned white for a few minutes.

"What do you think that was?" asked Annie.

Benny shrugged his broad shoulders. "Are you kidding me? I don't understand anything about this place. Your guess is as good as mine."

After the colors returned, the pair continued wandering about.

"What do you call it when you get a package from a mailman who's not very smart?" asked Benny.

"This is going to be bad," said Annie with a crooked half-smile.

"A special delivery."

She rolled her deep, brown eyes. "It was worse than bad."

"Okay, how about this one?" said Benny. Annie groaned. "No, no. It's a good one."

Annie looked at him doubtfully, and then waved her hand, silently granting permission to continue.

"This mailman comes up to a house. In front there's a boy and a huge, snarling dog. The mailman asks the boy, 'Does your dog bite?' The boy shakes his head and says 'no.' So the mailman tries to go to the door to deliver a package. Suddenly, the dog bites his leg and then runs off. The mailman is really angry and yells at the boy, 'I thought you said your dog doesn't bite.' The boy says, 'That wasn't my dog.'"

Hoping she could slow Benny's continuing prattle of bad jokes, Annie tried not to laugh, but she failed miserably. The humorous relief reminded her of feeling alive. And they both enjoyed the respite, until Sean suddenly appeared from the blackness without a glow.

For a moment, he moved his pale lips soundlessly, and then collapsed into his wife's arms.

* * *

"Benny," whispered Alyssa. "Are you okay?"

The big ghost's memories faded, returning him to the Dempsey family room.

"Yeah," he replied with a cloudy nod.

"Will and I are going to go out front for a couple minutes. I forgot what the sun looks like. We'll be back, okay?"

"Sure," replied Benny.

Fingers entwined, an exhausted Alyssa and Will staggered down the hall. Benny heard the front door creak open and close, and then he returned to his past.

* * *

Without sleep, calculating the uneven movement of time in the Nothing seemed impossible. For Benny, it felt like two days had passed before Sean spoke, again. During that spell, Sean lay still, making no sounds. He remained light-less, but his eyes were open, giving Annie and Benny some hope that he might wake from his trance. On separate occasions, each searched separately and unsuccessfully for Patrick, while the other remained behind with Sean.

Finally, in the midst of their silent vigil, when all hope seemed lost, Sean spoke.

"Annie," he said weakly, his head resting on his wife's lap.

"Sean!" she shouted with relief, squeezing him. "Are you okay? What happened?"

With a frail, broken voice, Sean explained how he and Patrick were near one of the red and white braids, when it descended toward them, hovering overhead an arm's length away. Both brothers reached out and touched the bands at the same time.

"I could feel the energy fill me and then I understood everything," said Sean. "Why we live. Why we die. Why we are in the Nothing." He closed his eyes. "I remember understanding, but I don't remember what I learned. It vanished so quickly and now there are only pieces," he added with frustration.

"Do you know how we get out of here?" Benny asked hopefully.

"I do," answered Sean, lifting himself into a sitting position. "This long wait for everyone is something that happened before. But it was okay again. The light was coming for me and for Patrick. To take us back. To start taking everyone back."

Annie and Benny exchanged hesitant glances as Sean slowly stood, rising like a worn, elderly man. He inspected himself, holding out his gloomy, unlit hands.

"My energy is gone," he continued. "It returned with the white streams. But I think a small part went into a red stream. And Patrick has it."

"What do you mean Patrick has it? What does he have?" she asked angrily.

Unfamiliar with an enraged Annie, Benny's furry eyebrows shot up, and he cautiously stepped backward.

"Touching the light released a loud, electric shock, and it threw us both down," recalled Sean. "When we recovered, a broken part of the red band was lying by our feet. It was a pulsing, shiny, red cylinder. Patrick picked it up, but then something happened. His face changed. It got dark and his glow changed from white to red. He looked at me like I was a stranger. And then he ran off, holding the broken red piece in his hand."

All three regarded each other, trying to make sense of their joint misfortune. Annie anxiously pulled back her hair, revealing the hidden half of her troubled face.

"But now," Sean finally added, "I don't think anyone can leave until that part of the red stream is returned. And worse, I don't think I can stay here."

"What?" shouted Annie and Benny.

Sean looked away. "I'm not sure how to explain why. I just know it. I must follow my energy. I have to go home."

This is not a good thing, thought Benny.

* * *

Sean's ominous words were quickly realized. His face aged rapidly, while his body weakened. Soon it was impossible for Sean to move without Annie's or Benny's assistance.

There were no reports of anyone leaving the Nothing. Worse, stories of strange things began spreading across the dark world. Rumors reached them about a man with some kind of dark-red, glowing rod, declaring he was in charge. Those opposing him were turned into wrinkled, soulless creatures, becoming members of a growing army. A day or so later, a short, white-haired old woman told Benny that the man's name was Patrick, and he carried a powerful wand called the Essence.

Sean asked questions as well. But others they met were leery of his aging face. He looked more and more like those they encountered and feared.

While Annie and Benny remained mystified and concerned by the developments, Sean's brooding became more pronounced as time passed. Finally, after the three received information that Patrick was looking for Sean, his silence ended.

"I need to speak with Annie," he told Benny. "Go to the red and white braid near the blue half-circle and we'll meet you there."

Staring at the twisted streams of light, Benny waited, thinking of his wife. He wondered whether days or months went by since he died, and whether she missed him. After they married, they waited a long time to have children, discovering that when they were ready they could not have them. The week before the accident, he and his wife had discussed adopting a baby. Now she was probably all alone.

I hope she finds someone, he thought as Sean and Annie arrived out of the Nothing.

"Benny, I'm going back," Sean announced, placing a reassuring hand on the mailman's shoulder.

"Going back?" asked Benny.

"Yes," said Sean stoically. "Back to a new life. I'm already sort of there."

"I don't understand," Benny replied, frowning. "You said you thought we can't go back until Patrick returns the piece of the red stream."

"I did. And I still think that. But my light is gone. It's started a new life. And because of that the streams want to take me back."

Benny's face twisted with confusion.

"Annie and I returned to this braid," Sean explained, pointing at the colored streams above them. "Each time they came down for me, but never for her. That makes me certain I was wrong. There's no part of me in what Patrick calls the Essence. Something else is happening."

"This is very weird," Benny said softly. "I don't understand anything. Being dead is more confusing than being alive."

"I know," replied Sean, facing his chubby companion. "Look, you need to be really careful. What Patrick has is very powerful. I think it might be the power of creation. And if I was the one to pick it up, I'd probably be as lost and crazy as he is now."

"So what's the plan?" asked Benny. "If you're going back, do Annie and I have your blessings for marriage?"

Annie smiled weakly. "You're funny, Benny," laughed Sean. "No. I prefer that you wait."

"Wait for what?"

"If you really want weird, here it is," said Sean. "You'll see me soon enough. Everything moves a lot faster where we came from. After I'm gone, Annie will fill you in on what I believe has happened and the plan to set things right. But do whatever you can to avoid Patrick. He's dangerous."

Eyes wide, Benny waited for more. Instead, Sean turned to his wife.

"Ready?" he asked.

Annie shook her head. "No."

Benny spun away, giving them a last moment. When he looked back, Sean stood a distance apart from Annie. The twisted streams overhead began dropping, white separating from red. The white light surrounded Sean, forming a huge, snowy bubble around his body. The darkness filled with the warm sound of a newborn's beating heart.

Sean's face softened and the lines upon it melted away. He fixed his eyes on those of his wife.

"Be patient and be smart," warned Sean, and then he faded, a pallid figure evaporating into a new life.

When the bubble disappeared, and the braided streams returned, Annie fell in by Benny's side, unexpectedly taking his hand. Her cold fingers frosted his palm.

"We met in third grade," she said flatly.

Benny waited, anticipating Annie's tears. None fell.

Chapter 4
Redemption

"And I'm your brother, Bradley. I'm Sean."

Bradley eyed Sean with suspicious disbelief.

"You're not my brother! You're lying!" Bradley shouted, waving his sword menacingly.

Sean closed the gap between them and narrowed his dark eyes. "Oh, really?"

"Yeah," replied Bradley, leaning in. "Really."

"So you're not the brother who punched me in the arm two weeks ago while I was taking a bath and then told Mom and Dad that you slipped and banged into me."

Bradley's misty mouth swung open with a breathless gasp.

"You're not the brother who took half of my Halloween candy last year," continued Sean, "and then burped in my face after you finished eating it."

"This is a trick," exclaimed Bradley.

"A trick," countered Sean, crossing his arms. "Like the kind of trick you played by pouring water on my sheets each night for a month to make me, Mom, and Dad think I was wetting the bed? Until they caught you doing it."

Bradley hovered about with his eyes cast downward. He received a huge punishment for that extended prank. No television or video games for six weeks. Worse, Sean started screaming and tattling anytime Bradley got near the family room.

But that was a four-year-old boy, not a man, thought Bradley.

"So why do you look like a grownup?"

"You see me the way I was. In my last life. Before I was your brother."

"Okay mister smarty-pants," said Bradley, perking up. "How do you have the same name? I mean, everyone here is worried about Sean. And that Sean is not my brother. That Sean is you."

"It's complicated," said Sean, suddenly preoccupied and staring behind Bradley. Red points of light now appeared in the distance.

Tracking Sean's concern, Bradley turned and stared into the Nothing. *Lost Souls*, he thought.

"Let's get moving," Sean announced urgently. Bradley hurried forward as Sean ran off.

"So what's the plan?" asked Bradley, continually peeking over his shoulder. The red lights were tracking them.

"You sound like Benny," answered Sean, peering upwards and following a white stream. "The plan is we go home."

"I don't think that's going to happen. The blue door or window or whatever it was blew up just before Annie ditched me," recalled Bradley. "We're not going home."

"Annie's taking care of that."

Annie? How did Annie get back in the middle of things, thought Bradley. More questions popped into his head, but one stuck out from the rest.

"Soooo," started Bradley. "Are you mad at me?"

Sean checked behind them. The red lights were closer and more appeared to their right. "I think we have other things to worry about at the moment."

"I mean," continued Bradley, "you're not so mad that you would think about leaving me here?"

Sean turned to the left. Red dots appeared in the distance in front of them. Bradley floated alongside him, anxiously waiting for an answer.

"I'm not leaving you," replied Sean, stopping and slowly turning in a circle. They were surrounded. Each dot was a blood stain in the night, growing larger and closer.

"You could be a little nicer," said Sean, confronting Bradley and ignoring their predicament for the moment.

"Definitely," said Bradley, nodding enthusiastically. "I will definitely be nicer."

"Let me play with your games," added Sean. Bradley nodded his head. "Play outside with me. Not make fun of me or call me names."

"Absolutely," agreed Bradley, raising a fluffy white hand. "I swear it."

Sean tilted his head indifferently. The red lights were closing in. And there was no sign of Annie. *At least we made it*, he thought, looking up.

"Whoa," said Bradley, finally realizing they were not moving. "What's going on?"

"We're here," replied Sean.

Bradley scanned the area. The only thing he saw was the Nothing, more Nothing, and even more Nothing, with Lost Souls rapidly approaching them from every direction.

"Oh yeah," Bradley said sarcastically. "Here. Hmm. How is this *here* different than any other *here*?"

"Over our heads is a braid of red and white streams of light. This is one of the places where the dead leave the Nothing to begin a new life. Right now it's not working."

Bradley gave a mocking nod. "Uh-huh. I can see why we stopped. And are you going to tell me why this braid thing I can't see isn't working?"

"The wand that I used to make pancakes and the purple apple and the bicycle is a piece of red light. About five years ago of our time, or actually Dempsey time, it broke off when I was here and still dead. That piece of red light is what everyone calls the Essence."

"Oh. Now, everything is clear," said Bradley. "Not!"

In the distance the points of light were broadening into figures. Bradley tucked in closer to Sean and waited.

"So what's the plan?" he repeated.

"Stay quiet and let me talk."

As the fiery red-cloaked Lost Souls arrived, wearing angry, wrinkled faces, Sean raised his hand to greet them. While they circled, Bradley picked out Cade, Kir, and Wallace, the last of whom stepped forward. Bradley squeaked and tried hiding behind Sean, prompting snickers from some of the Lost Souls.

"What is going on?" demanded Sean.

"You only get to fool us once, Sean," replied Wallace

with equal severity, while casting a reproachful glance at Cade. "Patrick is coming. See if you can fool him."

"Let's pin the kid," said Kir. "Patrick just wants Sean. We can have some fun while we wait."

"We're not doing anything until he gets here," announced Wallace. "Is that understood?"

The Lost Souls nodded their heads submissively. But Sean smiled with satisfaction and pointed past Wallace.

In the distance, a wide flare of red and white rushed toward the circle. With static crackles, each flash blazed upward, turning the Nothing's horizon into sunset amber. The Lost Souls and Bradley recoiled as Annie appeared, shouting a war cry and holding the radiant Essence over her head like a torch-bearer. She burst into the circle hollering, then fell toward Sean with an outstretched arm. Annie slipped to one knee before her husband caught her. Sean took the Essence in his hands as she slid to his side.

Bradley hurried back to Sean and Annie. "Okay, you jerks," he announced to the Lost Souls, raising his *Hero Warrior* sword. "Don't even think of messing with me and my brother."

No one responded. All eyes, including Annie's, as she struggled back to her feet, fixed on Sean holding the Essence. It pulsed in his hands, fading back and forth between crimson and brilliant white. The smell of saltwater ocean and electric sparks filled the illuminated void.

"Are you good?" asked Annie, pushing dangling streaks of dark hair from her face.

Sean nodded. "Yeah. I see it, Annie. I see him. I see us. I see all of them," said Sean, gazing at the Lost Souls. He turned to his wife. "But no craziness. He's wrapped around it."

"I don't understand," she replied.

"Patrick's wrapped around the Essence," said Sean, trying to explain. "It's protecting me."

The Lost Souls crept forward. Defensively, Sean raised the Essence over his head. Above them, the red and white braid brightened in response.

"I see them," yelled Bradley, looking up. "I see the streams!"

Sean eyed the young, wrinkled faces around him. A new feeling infused their sad, withered features. Their soulless eyes filled with collective hope, desperately seeking a lost spirit.

"I can give it back to you," Sean said to the Lost Souls. With a whispering hum, the Essence vibrated in his hands. "I can give it back!"

Wallace stepped forward. "Patrick said we needed your light."

"You don't. I have yours. I have your soul and I can give it back," repeated Sean, struggling to hold on to the Essence as it purred louder and grew brighter.

"Then save me," begged Wallace. "Please. Before Patrick comes."

"And me," said Kir, joining Wallace. "Save me."

The other Lost Souls united in an anxious chorus, pleading for deliverance. Bradley floated to Annie, and they watched Sean slowly begin swinging the Essence overhead in large circles. A matching cone filled the space above. Two streams of light emerged, reaching toward the braid until the luminous objects fused into a brilliant funnel of cascading, waterless falls. The red streams quickly receded, leaving the white ones, bathed in the soft sound of beating hearts beckoning the Lost Souls to them.

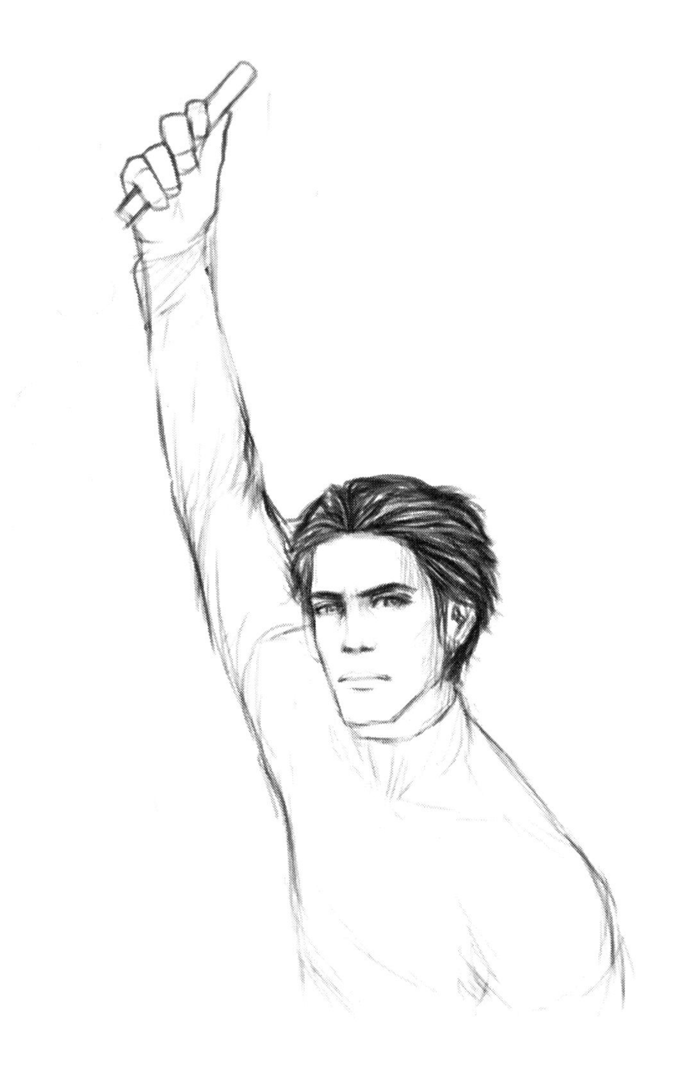

“It’s beautiful,” whispered Bradley, drifting toward the gentle sound.

Annie jumped in his path, blocking him. “Hold on,” she warned. “You’re not going anywhere.”

One by one, the Lost Souls entered the white channel. A glowing bubble formed, surrounding their bodies and washing away the unsightly lines scarring their faces. Each Lost Soul rose, slowly dissolving and smiling with salvation. Just before vanishing, a small vibrating string of white light unwound out of the Essence, lifting away from Sean and trailing after its owner.

Wallace was last. His eager, charcoal eyes shifted to Sean.

"Thank you," he said. "And I'm sorry," he added, turning to Bradley, who accepted the apology with a slight nod.

When Wallace was gone, the lights above faded. Sean lowered the Essence and it returned to a subdued, soundless, crimson glow. Exhausted, he closed his eyes, collecting himself for a moment.

"Where did they go?" asked Bradley.

"To new lives," replied Annie. Realizing the real danger remained, she searched the veiled blackness. Her eyes fixed on one place. Bradley swiveled and saw three red dots.

"I hate red dots," he said.

Annie moved to her recovering husband's side. "It's Patrick."

Sean opened his eyes and faced his wife. "Bradley and I need to go home."

Chapter 5
Brothers

"What?" shouted Annie.

"We have to go," said Sean.

"No! You have the Essence. I didn't go crazy touching it. You didn't go crazy. Wish it away."

Bradley retreated, unwilling to interrupt. He recognized the same sounds of his parents fighting and realized it was best to stay quiet until the storm blew over.

"Annie. We didn't go crazy because some part of Patrick is wrapped around the Essence and that's stopping me from going as nuts as he did. All I think I can do is the same thing I did back home. Make pancakes, bikes, and purple apples."

"But the braid came –"

"The braid came down in response to this," explained Sean, firmly holding the red, glowing Essence. "I just lifted it up. I didn't make anything happen."

Annie cemented her hands to her hips. "I thought the whole plan was to destroy the Essence, reunite with him, and be done with this place!"

"It is, but not here. After holding the Essence, I'm certain Patrick is dangerous in the Nothing, with or without it. He thinks he needs the Essence, but he is infused with the red stream having held it for so long. We have to get Patrick through and then try. It's too risky here. If I make a wish in the Nothing and it doesn't work, Patrick will have the Essence again. And then we'll never be able to accomplish our plan."

Annie shook her head. "A long time ago, you said there was one big danger. Touching the Essence. You did that as a boy again in a new life. You did that here, just now. And you're still okay."

Sean stepped toward her, but Annie curled away, looking down.

"Forget about the danger," said Sean. "If I make a wish here and it actually works, Bradley will lose a brother. His parents will lose a son. How can I let that happen?"

Annie lifted her head and, for the first time since he met her, Bradley saw a trembling face filled with welling sadness.

"But what about us?" she asked almost inaudibly. "What about what we lost?"

Sean had no answer. Spotting the same lull in his parents' fights, and seeing the size of the red lights growing as they moved toward them, Bradley decided it was time to speak.

"Look," he said. "I have no idea what the heck you guys are talking about. But if that's Patrick, he's getting closer. So I'm thinking we should go."

Annie led the way through the darkness, with Sean quietly at her side. Bradley glided behind them, twirling in circles occasionally, enjoying his remaining time as a ghost. Waving his white wispy sword, he looked forward to playing *Hero Warrior* after proving his valor by defeating the Shriek. *I am your loyal servant,* thought Bradley, imagining the aging king's face.

The pale, indigo glow of an oval-shaped portal appeared ahead. "I thought it blew up," said Bradley.

"It's a new one," replied Annie over her shoulder. "It's the mirror in your family room."

Awesome, thought Bradley. *Right by the television!*

When they reached the blue gateway, Sean stopped, leveling a serious stare at the white, wispy teenager. *Oh, no*, Bradley worried silently. *He's going to leave me here.*

"You and I are going through," Sean said firmly. "And when we do I'm just your little brother, again. I'll remember our lives, and things that happened to Sean Dempsey, even Annie and Benny bringing me the Essence. But I probably won't remember any of what's happened in the Nothing. It's not part of my life as your brother."

Bradley's cloudy eyes flashed relief.

"That doesn't mean you can break your promise," added Sean, noting his brother's reaction. "Is that understood?"

"Understood," replied Bradley with an obligatory nod.

Sean looked behind the boy. Patrick was quickly closing in.

"Now, listen. Annie is going to let Patrick through. Once he's in our house, I have to wish the wand away, forever."

"Sounds good to me," said Bradley, smiling.

"You have to find a way to get me to make that wish."

Bradley shuddered. His little brother Sean hated him and loved the glass wand. *I'll never get him to wish it away*, he thought.

Sean stepped toward his brother. "Find a way, Bradley," he repeated. "You can do it."

"I'll try."

"Good. Now, go through. I'll be there in a minute."

Bradley hesitated, glancing from Sean to Annie. There was little to like about this dark, uncertain world, but these were the only adults around. He now relied upon them, but if just Sean followed, it would be only three kids and Benny against Patrick.

I don't like those odds, he thought.

"Go through," Sean said urgently.

"All right," Bradley replied reluctantly. He turned to Annie. "Bye."

Bradley whirled in a circle. "Flying!" he cried and then dove into the blue portal.

Sean faced his wife. There was no time for a long goodbye or heartfelt declarations. He could only offer Annie a short message of hope for them. It was something he discovered while connected to the red and white streams, freeing the Lost Souls, but at the same time recognizing new conception awaiting spirits from beyond the physical world. When he finished, Annie's lips split into an awkward smile.

"That would be really weird," she responded.

"I don't think so. A little different," he added with a smile. "Okay?"

"Okay," said Annie. "Assuming you're still alive," she noted with concern.

"Yep," replied Sean stoically. "Assuming I'm still alive."

They leaned in and kissed for the last time. Gripping the Essence tightly, Sean twisted away, plunging into the blue doorway and out of the Nothing.

Annie walked to the other side of the mirror's entrance, hiding behind the glowing membrane between life and death. Soon after, Patrick and the two Lost Souls arrived.

"Follow me," she heard Patrick say. And then silence.

I got him again, thought Annie with a satisfied grin. Leaping up, she rushed around the portal and closed the pathway home.

* * *

Bradley and his plastic sword fell from the mirror with a loud thump, toppling to the carpeted floor. Alyssa, seated on the couch next to Will, bolted up and rushed to her brother.

"Bradley!" she cried out. "Are you okay? What happened? Where's Sean? What's going on?"

"Will you let go of me," complained Bradley, shaking off his sister's hug.

"Where's Annie? Where's Sean?" asked Benny, drifting over to them.

I already miss the Nothing, thought Bradley. "Will you both keep quiet?" he demanded, scurrying to his feet. "Sean's coming through in a second. He's talking to Annie."

"What do you mean he's talking to Annie," yelled Alyssa. "How could you leave your little brother inside there?"

"He's not so little in there," said Bradley, aiming a fierce, blue-eyed stare at Benny. "Or did marshmallow here forget to mention that?"

Alyssa shot Benny a questioning glance. "There may be some things I forgot to tell you," admitted the ghost, his fluffy fingers steepled and tapping nervously.

Further explanations were postponed as four-year-old Sean popped through the mirror, clutching the glass wand in his hand. He landed on his feet, stumbling for a moment, but keeping his balance.

"Again," he shouted, waving the Essence in the air. "Again, Alyssa, please?"

Alyssa released Bradley and scooped her younger brother into her arms. "Sean! Oh my God," she exclaimed with tears springing down her cheeks. "I missed you, buddy."

"I guess you didn't miss me that much," muttered Bradley.

He raised his sword and surveyed the room. Alyssa lifted her arm to take the Essence from Sean, but Bradley swatted her hand away.

"Sean needs to keep that, and we need to move away from the mirror. Trust me, get back."

"Patrick?" asked Benny softly.

Bradley nodded and Benny swiftly slid backward. On her knees, Alyssa crawled away from the mirror, clutching Sean. They all formed a feeble military line, a ghost at one end, Alyssa at the other, her arm wrapped around Sean, and a thirteen-year-old in the middle, bearing his plastic sword. Will remained on the couch, anxious and perplexed.

"Do you remember anything?" asked Bradley, turning to Sean.

Sean slid out of his sister's arm, considering the question. "Look both ways," he said finally.

"No," complained Bradley. "Anything about Patrick? About the mirror?"

Sean beamed. "It's a ride. You go in upstairs and come down here."

"Who's Patrick?" offered Will nervously.

As if summoned, the mirror shimmered and Patrick entered the Dempsey family room, followed by two Lost Souls. In the well-lit room, the Lost Souls were even more frightening than they appeared to Alyssa the night before. Their seamless, scarlet clothes burned brightly, and their faces were covered with long, seared scars. Each had straight, jet-black hair.

Are they vampires? Alyssa wondered, inching backward.

Patrick was now a ghost, a crimson figure billowing fiercely in the air. But his stony, square jaw and dark, evil eyes were no less fearsome. As Patrick floated toward them, the Dempseys and Benny withdrew a step.

"The gang is all here," he announced, flashing a nasty grin.

Behind him, the Lost Souls cackled. "Yeah," said one, moving to Patrick's side. "The gang is all here."

Patrick shook his head, and Bradley wondered if he would lash out at his companion. But the red ghost spotted Sean and the Essence.

"If you don't mind, little boy," Patrick said, "I would like that back."

"Yeah," repeated the same Lost Soul. "If you don't mind he would like –"

The same hissing Alyssa and Benny heard the night before filled the family room. Their eyes flashed to the mirror and saw their reflection as both Lost Souls evaporated with a muted scream. The startling disappearance prompted a slew of four-letter profanity flowing unchecked from Will's mouth. Benny and the Dempsey children turned to Alyssa's boyfriend, who was riveted to the couch.

"He said bad words," declared Sean.

"Wonderful," said Patrick, smirking and ignoring Will.

"You're all alone," Benny said protectively, shifting himself in front of Alyssa and Sean. "We have the Essence and all you have is the Nothing."

"Aren't you the smart one, fat man," replied Patrick insolently. "That mirror won't stop me from going back. And when I'm ready, I'll return with things a lot scarier than Lost Souls."

The fearsome ghost rolled his head toward Bradley and pointed a blood-red finger at him.

"But first," Patrick continued, "I'll be sure to get rid of your girlfriend. She's the one that's all alone now."

"You have a girlfriend?" asked Sean.

Bradley looked down at his little brother. "Sean. Wish away the wand. Wish it away."

The boy gripped the Essence tighter. He liked it. It made him pancakes and a bike. It made him happy. He shook his head vigorously at Bradley.

"You're wasting your time and my time," said Patrick, creeping forward. "Don't listen to him, Sean. Do you really want to wish away something you love so much? I love it too. It was made for me. And it was made for you, Sean. You're the only one in this house that can make wishes with it. You're special and now he wants you to make it go away."

"Leave him alone," said Benny defiantly, moving between Patrick and Sean.

"I can make wishes with it, too," continued Patrick, peeking around the chubby ghost. "If you give it to me, I can make a very special wish for you."

Bradley knelt in front of Sean and jammed his sword into the carpet. "Sean. I am the Hero Warrior, your loyal servant."

Sean's apple-red cheeks brightened. "Really?"

"You are my lord and my king, Sean. Wish the wand

away, and I will always be your loyal servant."

Patrick spat out a nervous laugh. "He can't wish it away. If Sean destroys the wand, he'll be destroyed, as well."

"No he won't," said Bradley, rising with his sword outstretched. "He's not your brother anymore. He's my brother. And you are just a ghost."

Patrick's burning face recoiled, but his black eyes bulged furiously.

"Give it back!" he lashed out at them. "Give it back now or I will kill Annie!"

Waves of red light burst from Patrick's mouth, roaring across the room. The furniture lifted and shook violently, tossing Will off the couch and onto the floor. Patrick paused, gauging the effect his outburst caused.

I don't need the wand, Patrick realized triumphantly. *I still have its power!*

"I like Annie," said Sean defiantly, holding out the Essence. "But I don't like you. I wish this away, forever."

Chapter 6
Returns

The red clouds forming Patrick darkened and solidified into a starlit mass of shimmering black. A dark column hung in the air, joined by the Essence which flew from Sean's hand. The cut glass of the wand faded, becoming a similar but much smaller black rod, sparkling with tiny points of light.

Sounds of trickling water rose from the two glistening objects, filling the family room as Alyssa, Bradley, Sean, Benny, and Will circled around them. The noise rose to a cascading roar, ending with the black outer skin peeling away from each object, falling and then disappearing into the carpet with a dry splash.

A pair of entwined, pulsating, red and white threads hung suspended in the air. The larger filaments that were Patrick separated, swirling and unwinding like two strands of DNA. The small red thread of what was the Essence unwound, but the white strand broke apart, forming tiny pale strings, too numerous to count.

Lost Souls, thought Bradley, watching the small, beating, white lines dance slowly around the red one.

The mirror on the wall shifted, losing its reflection. Annie's face appeared through the shimmering surface, but only for a moment. She was immediately thrown back with force into the Nothing as all of the energy strands, with the exception of the long white filament, rushed forward between Benny and Alyssa, diving through the black membrane with a loud, electric crack.

The remaining white thread, all that was left of Patrick, hovered for one final moment, the top bending and twisting as if searching for an escape. Its thin head settled on Sean and burst toward the young boy, shooting into his small chest. A white explosion of a hundred camera flashes blinded the circle of onlookers, spinning their heads away. When Alyssa and Bradley's eyesight recovered, they were still standing. The white strand was gone, and Sean lay lifeless on the floor.

* * *

Sprawled out in the darkness, Annie found a path to consciousness following the soft hum of the open portal by her feet. Her eyes fluttered and she pushed aside some mental cobwebs, checking to see if she was in one piece. Apart from knocking Annie out, the blast of energy returning to the Nothing had left her unscathed.

Sean, thought Annie suddenly.

Pushing through the soft blue barrier, she entered the Dempsey family room, finding Sean motionless in Alyssa's arms. The teenage girl was weeping softly, while Benny, Bradley, and Will leaned in with concern. Benny lifted his head as Annie floated over and he saw the fear on her sheer, ashen face.

"He's breathing," Benny said reassuringly.

Annie dipped in close to the floor. Alyssa's glistening tears dotted Sean's placid cheeks.

"Will he be okay?" she asked desperately.

"Give him some time," replied Annie in a soothing tone. She turned to Benny. "Patrick's energy?"

"The red went back," said Benny. "The white went into Sean."

Alyssa, Bradley and even Will watched the ghosts. Not understanding what happened, they each projected a silent demand for an explanation.

Annie began by recounting the story of how Patrick, Sean, Benny, and she died together and came to the Nothing. Alyssa's eyes widened when she realized Annie was describing the same Sean that she held in her arms. Annie continued, talking about their white glow, their search for a way out, what had happened to Patrick and Sean at the braid, and how Patrick had disappeared into the Nothing with the splintered piece of red energy.

"I thought you said the two brothers created the Essence to escape," Alyssa said, staring at Benny.

"There may be some things I made up," admitted Benny with white, apologetic eyes.

Annie continued, describing how Sean aged and the Lost Souls appeared. And then she spoke of Sean confiding in her what he believed was the real problem, and his plan to fix it.

"He thought the best way to end everything was to go back. To be born again. And when he was old enough, to have us lure Patrick here to make them one."

"Make them one?" Alyssa asked. "Patrick is inside my brother?"

"No," replied Annie quietly. "Sean and Patrick were identical twins. They shared the same soul. That may not always be true of twins, but it is for them. Or it was."

Annie ran a cloudy finger across Sean's face. Her husband was gone forever, replaced by a child having no memories of their first glance, their first kiss, and all the moments making up their lives together.

"I know you have a lot of questions," continued Annie. "But I don't know all of the answers. Sean felt most of them intuitively, but he was never certain. To be honest, I prefer that some of the truth remain a mystery. You already learned too much about death, which can't be a good thing for the living."

"You have to tell us why his name is Sean," pressed Bradley. "That's really weird. I mean our mom named him that. He didn't show up with a tag on him that said 'Sean.'"

"I know," Annie replied, her pale lips drawing a small smile. "Sean existed in both places because half of his soul was in Patrick. The power of that is very strong. I can only guess it creates ideas like the one your mom had when she decided on a name. It certainly pushed Sean through the mirror to find the other part of who he was."

"But he's not evil now, right?" asked Alyssa.

"No. Sean's not evil. He's a little boy. And the real Patrick wasn't evil. You never met that person. But you will. They are one, again."

Sean stirred in his sister's lap, and Alyssa sucked in a breath. "Oh my God," she whispered. "Sean? Buddy?"

"Give him a few moments," Annie chided.

"So why did Sean leave us when I came through?" asked Bradley. "Why did he say he was going off to look for my brother?"

"That was the plan. He went to look for Patrick and lure him back to your home. But after the portal was destroyed, I left you behind to find Sean and figure out what we should do," explained Annie. "And you know the rest, Bradley. You were very brave."

Blushing, Bradley looked down. For reasons he could not comprehend, he suddenly thought of Miranda Stevens, the girl who asked him to have lunch.

I wonder if she thinks I'm brave.

"How did you steal the Essence from Patrick?" asked Alyssa. "I mean, he was pretty nasty and the Lost Souls must have been everywhere."

"Hmm," replied Annie with a sinful grin. "I'll let your imagination figure out how a woman could pry even the most prized possession from a man's hand."

Benny whistled loudly, and now it was Alyssa's turn to blush.

"Alyssa," squeaked Sean, opening his pastel-blue eyes. "Is he gone?"

"Yes," cried Alyssa, sweeping her little brother up. "He's gone forever, buddy. Forever and ever."

Annie peered over at Benny. It was time to leave, and he nodded knowingly.

"Annie," said Sean softly. "I made the wand go away. I'm sorry."

"That's all right, sweetie. You did a good thing."

Alyssa watched Annie's eyes trail away, and she was certain she saw tiny, puffy tears dotting the ghost's face. Annie joined Benny and faced the group.

"We need to go now," she announced. The children, including a wobbly Sean, rose quickly with her words. "I think you may want to keep all of this to yourselves. I don't imagine any adult is going to believe you anyway. It will just be your crazy little secret."

They nodded in agreement, particularly Will, who bobbed his head forcefully.

"Will we ever see you guys again?" asked Bradley.

Benny gazed hopefully at Annie. "Maybe," she said in a mild, mysterious voice. "You never know what the future holds."

The two ghosts glided to the mirror. Annie hesitated at the black, liquid boundary. Her soft, white shoulders rose and fell with a silent sigh.

She's afraid to look back, thought Alyssa.

"Goodbye, Annie," whispered Sean, breaking the silence.

"Goodbye, Sean," said Annie with her head fixed forward. Unseen, she mouthed the words "I love you," and then leapt through.

Benny intended to break the somber mood that enveloped the family room. The big ghost drifted in front of the children, cleared his transparent throat, and bowed.

"Want to see a magic trick?" he asked slyly.

All four members of his audience nodded. Benny began bobbing up and down in rhythm, as if he was jumping rope.

"Tell me," he announced formally, while bouncing in front of them. "How do you make a teenager jump?"

Bradley raised his hand. "Give him a basketball?"

"Nope," said Benny. "Anybody else?"

"With a magic wand?" asked Sean.

"No, sir," replied Benny. "And no more magic wands for you, my young friend. Do you give up?"

The group nodded. With a burst of speed, Benny lurched toward Will and shouted "Boo!" Will soared backward on to the couch, crashing down in the cushions, clutching his heart. Benny swiveled around to the Dempsey children with a huge smile.

"Ta da!" he shouted, and bowed once more. "Now, that's magic!"

The Dempsey children applauded. Will remained where he landed, his hands affixed to the center of his chest. Benny winked at Alyssa.

"Goodbye, girlfriend."

With a ghostly whoosh, Benny followed Annie and disappeared, leaving Alyssa, Bradley, and Sean behind, watching as their reflections returned for good.

* * *

Two hours later, Estelle Watson slowly made her way upstairs to her bedroom, intent on taking an afternoon nap. She was surprised to find her three cats, Minnie, Dusty, and Rascal, bundled and sleeping soundly together on the small area rug by her nightstand.

Finally, she thought. *They're done staring at that crazy house.*

Mrs. Watson intended to speak with Mrs. Dempsey about whatever those children were doing that inflicted such feline distress. She would demand an explanation.

In the Dempsey home, three children lay similarly bundled together on the same couch where Will had cowered earlier. Alyssa showed her shell-shocked boyfriend out of their house shortly after the drama ended, offering Will a kiss on the cheek and a promise to see him that night. The Dempsey children then formulated a plan to clean up as much as they could before their parents returned. At the conclusion of their brief meeting, Bradley suggested a quick power nap first, to which Alyssa and Sean agreed. Ninety-six minutes later, they were still asleep.

Neither Mrs. Watson's cats, nor the Dempsey children, heard the car door close, the front door open, or the footsteps echoing down the hall. With arms crossed, John and Leslie Dempsey looked from the kitchen table to their sleeping children and back again.

"Hey! What's with the pancakes?"

Epilogue

Leslie Dempsey sits in the garden behind her home, watching her children enjoying a sunny, summer afternoon. Three years have passed since the day she discovered her pregnancy. Soon afterward, Leslie learned she was carrying twins.

Her doctor and her husband worried about how Leslie would hold up delivering and raising two babies this late in life. But the "older" mom held up. John and the kids were wonderfully supportive, especially Bradley who, to Leslie's surprise, regularly helped her around the house since she gave birth. Even Sean lent a hand.

All three children were insistent about the babies' names, and they took to the little ones from the first day the new family of seven was united at the hospital. It was as if the family was always this large.

Leslie watches Alyssa and Bradley running around with their brother, who points at the birds and squirrels. Nearby, Sean strolls through the summer blossoms with his little sister, her hand gripping his finger, tugging him along to visit the next flower.

Their mother reflects on how different those two souls are compared with the other three.

Alyssa and Bradley have their Benny, thinks Leslie.

But Annie has her Sean.

THE END?

Acknowledgements

This self-published author relied heavily on his editors. So I begin my acknowledgements with the Region III Book Club, who collectively read the earliest copy of my manuscript, providing corrections and comments. In particular, I thank Tony Cho for his thoughts early in the process and Tony Tarone for helping me clarify the most important parts of Book III.

Bruce DuBoff earns the title of Editor-in-Chief. Brandishing an experienced red pen, he helped me cut out the grammatical garbage and taught me the fine art of polishing each sentence. The sights, sounds, tastes, and scents of this tale evolved to higher forms as a result of his guidance.

Krystle Carkeek transformed my words into three exquisite covers and thirty-seven wonderful sketches – a huge effort! Her images created a beautiful, visual connection for all readers. And she agreed to participate as my digital partner in this endeavor, rather than for hire. I am forever grateful.

On the technical side, Art Lassin (www.lassindesign.com) joined the team as our designer. Krystle's covers became the professional faces of the Essence thanks to Art's contributions – and he also delivered the very cool E3 logo. In New Zealand, Lis Sowerbutts (www.diypublishing.co.nz) formatted the word-processing files into digital ones for Amazon, Nook, and iBooks. She was always cheerful and responsive. Closer to home, Garrett Love and Studio16Media (www.studio16media) created the Essence website, combining all the varying elements of the book to create a uniform image for the surfers.

I conclude the acknowledgements with the following unordered list of Thank Yous:

- To Brett for his dream, to Danielle for her pen, and to Janet forever
- My parents, the unconditional creators of my creativity
- Allen and Bettyruth, for their safety net of love and support
- David, Michael, and the beach of our childhood
- Lewis Katz and Ron Rubin, for lifting me up
- Savannah, my first reader
- Eddie, my most fanatical reader
- Eric, Tony, "Lightning" Lacko, and the rest of the Cook team
- Gail, who said "just write"
- Al-Can, for being there when others ran for cover
- Mr. Flatley, the guy who purportedly taught me bad habits
- Albert, for your first read and all of our shared laughter
- Tammy, Amanda, and chapter summaries at lunch
- All card-carrying members of Jay's Basement
- The World Boardgaming Championships, my summer home
- Patton Oswalt and your inspiring Laughspin keynote address
- and to Amazon, Nook, and iTunes, for giving new authors a welcome home

ABOUT THE AUTHOR

Raised by wolves after being abandoned by his parents in the northern Minnesota wilderness, Vel Grande taught himself to read using the journals of lost hikers eaten by his pack. When he is not writing, Vel enjoys board gaming and howling at the stars while travelling the open road at night. *The Essence – A Ghost Story in Three Days* is his first book series.

ABOUT THE ILLUSTRATOR

Krystle Carkeek, a student living in Cherry Hill, New Jersey, is looking forward to studying engineering. She is also an aspiring artist and draws in her free time. Krystle started painting in her freshman year of high school and has been passionate about it ever since.

FOR MORE INFORMATION
VISIT ALYSSA, BRADLEY, SEAN AND THE BUDDIES AT

www.aghoststoryin3days.com

Made in the USA
Middletown, DE
16 September 2016